The Volcano Ogre

Books by *Lin Carter*

PUBLISHED BY DOUBLEDAY

The Adventures of Zarkon, Lord of the Unknown:

THE NEMESIS OF EVIL

INVISIBLE DEATH

THE VOLCANO OGRE

Fantasy Anthologies:

KINGDOMS OF SORCERY

REALMS OF WIZARDRY

Science Fiction Novels:

THE VALLEY WHERE TIME STOOD STILL

Zarkon,
LORD OF THE UNKNOWN
IN

The Volcano Ogre

A CASE FROM THE FILES OF OMEGA,

AS TOLD TO
LIN CARTER

DOUBLEDAY & COMPANY, INC.
GARDEN CITY, NEW YORK
1976

All of the characters in this book
are fictitious, and any resemblance
to actual persons, living or dead,
is purely coincidental.

Library of Congress Cataloging in Publication Data

Carter, Lin.
Zarkon, Lord of the Unknown in the volcano ogre.

I. Title. II. Title: The volcano ogre.
PZ4.C3239Zat [PS3553.A7823] 813'.5'4
ISBN 0-385-08807-8
Library of Congress Catalog Card Number 75-21217

Printed in the United States of America
First Edition

Contents

For Kendall Foster Crossen,
the creator of the Green Lama.

NOTE:

On the following pages you will find my novelization of the case reported in Omega File 17. The events described here took place during the month of April 1971.

I would like to emphasize that which perhaps does not even require pointing out. I mean, that what follows has been very heavily fictionalized.

I wrote this novelization from photostat copies of the notes on the case recorded in File 17, and from about three hours' total interview-time with those members of the Omega organization who partook therein and who were available at the time of this writing, early 1975. Since I don't have a tape recorder memory like Doc Jenkins, I had to actually use a tape recorder.

While the events described in these pages really took place more or less as I describe them, obviously an element of fictionalization had to enter into my account. I don't know what some of the people on Rangatoa looked like, for instance. And, not having been on the spot, I have been forced to imagine such thing as descriptions of the island, the scenes of the events, the tones of voice used, and the expressions on people's faces, and so on. My dialogue is almost entirely invention: but accurate invention, I hope, based on informed and calculated guesses as to what the characters in this book might have said to each other under the reported circumstances.

Under the terms of my agreement with Omega, all of the personal and place names in this book are my invention. While these people all actually lived, none of their true names are even remotely similar to the names I have given them. This is also true of the locale of the story. There is no such island as Rangatoa in the Pacific Ocean, no chain of islands called the Luzon Group, no such island confederation as the Luzon Union, no capital city named Mantilla, and so on. (In fact, I borrowed some of these names from one of Lester Dent's Doc Savage novels, called *Pirate of the Pacific.*)

Prince Zarkon and his five lieutenants and their Omega group actually exist. But their organization is not called Omega, neither is it located where I suggest it is, nor are their true names the same as those I have given them. The man I have decided to call Prince Zarkon makes every attempt to avoid publicity, rather than striving for it. While it is quite true that he and his organization are devoted to the battle against supercrime, the secrecy with which the Omega organization surrounds itself helps to protect it from those who would destroy it.

Those who are in need of help would be advised to look elsewhere for assistance. It is perhaps not generally known, but every large American city contains a local office of the FBI, which is plainly listed in the telephone book. If you need help, seek it from the proper authorities.

This is the third of the cases I have selected from the files of Omega for novelization. Naturally, I have chosen the more fantastic and colorful of the many cases undertaken by this extraordinary organization. Next to Z5 itself, which is, after all, semiofficial, it is generally conceded to be the best and most superlatively efficient private crime-fighting organization in the world today. Part of the reason for its phenomenal success is that it operates in almost complete secrecy; very few in the Underworld learn of its very existence until too late.

For that reason, neither I nor my publishers will pass along to Omega any mail from my readers. I have already had to return over one hundred letters from readers seeking the aid of Zarkon of Omega.

Those desperately in need of Omega's help should take an advertisement in the personal columns of the Knickerbocker City *Daily Sentinel,* and should begin their ad with the code phrase *Zelda: please contact Box —. Important!*

A few notes and observations:

The Cobalt Club exists, and is as I have described it, for Prince Zarkon has taken me there as his guest. However, the rather exclusively legendary membership of the club (for those readers able to see beyond a last name) is only my whimsical sense of humor, which at times is irrepressible.

The battle between Wakuaha and the fire devil, who still sleeps beneath Mount Rangatoa, is a genuine Polynesian legend. Those who would like to know more about it should consult Copeland's *Polynesian Mythology,* published in 1906 but still the recognized authority.

The secret of the manufacture of the polymerized-glass fiber, and the technique of vacuum-bubble insulation, both mentioned in this book, were believed to have been lost with the death of their inventor, as described herein. By a rather amusing coincidence, however, even as this volume goes to press a news story in the issue of the New York *Times* dated April 1, 1975, reports that the Hazzard Laboratories at College Point, Long Island, have rediscovered the secret process and are manufacturing the miracle fabric.

—LIN CARTER

P.S. I am greatly indebted to Señor Juan Mindoro II, senior vice-president of the Luzon Islands Tourist Office at 9 Rockefeller Plaza, New York City, for his kind generosity in supplying me with color slides, movie travelogue footage, brochures, and a geological survey map of Rangatoa Island, for my research in writing this book.

Without his cooperation, it would have been much more difficult for me to describe the foliage, native village, volcano, and general scenery of the island in those scenes and chapters which take place on Rangatoa.

—LC

The Volcano Ogre

CHAPTER 1

The Burning Troll

Tarapaho is the largest town on the small Pacific island of Rangatoa. It is also the *only* town on the island.

It is built along the curved beach of the lagoon, a double row of bamboo huts which march side-by-side the length of the town's only street, which is a broad lane of beaten earth. This dirt road, at its further end, terminates at the steps leading to Tarapaho's largest and most imposing building, a two-story trading post maintained by Señor Felipe Valdez, the island's most prominent citizen. At the other end it dwindles away into a smooth beach of coral sand, where a dock extends out into the blue waters of the Pacific, lazing under a golden morning sun.

Outrigger canoes were drawn up onto this beach, and a small schooner was anchored off the end of this dock.

Scrawny chickens scratched in the dirt between the huts of the town. A mongrel dog or two slept under the steps to the trading post.

No one, as yet, was abroad. Yesterday evening the people of Tarapaho had held a feast in celebration of the local independence day, the anniversary of the date on which Rangatoa, and the other islands of the group to which it belonged, had won their independence from Spain. Date wine had flowed rather freely, and a whole pig had been roasted in a sandpit on the beach, and the girls of Rangatoa had danced the local equivalent of the hula. Joy, as the saying has it, had been unconfined. So had the supply of drinkables. In honor of the occasion, Felipe Valdez had taken the schooner to a larger island in the chain and brought back a case of Philippino beer and two cases of hard liquor. As a result of the imbibement of these potables, few of the citizens of Tarapaho were astir at this hour.

Which explains why nobody saw Tommy Kahua leave his hut at the end of town and start up the bamboo-covered hills in the direction of the mountain.

Tommy's outrigger was the long one with the ornate carvings on the prow. He was one of the best fishermen on the island, and usually feasted on his own catch, selling the rest to Señor Valdez, who took it to the larger islands and returned with crisp golden banknotes bearing the seal of the National Bank of Luzon.

But all of the previous afternoon, the succulent and mouth-watering odors of the roasting pig had caressed the nostrils of Tommy Kahua. Roast pig was, he reminded himself, a rare delicacy, and far tastier, on the whole, than even fresh-caught fish. So, in early evening before sundown, and before the celebration began, he had planted home-made traps around the slopes of Mount Rangatoa, where wild pigs were sometimes seen. And this morning he was up bright and early, despite a throbbing brow, to see if Dame Chance had replenished his larder.

Although Tommy Kahua could not have guessed it, this was a serious mistake.

And it was the last mistake Tommy Kahua would ever make.

Mount Rangatoa was an active volcano of rather modest proportions, less than a thousand feet high. A plume of snowy vapors crowned its jagged crest, which could be seen for miles out to sea like a gigantic feather from a roc's wing. Hence its name, for *rangatoa* in the Luaua dialect means "white feather."

There was no particular danger in living in such close proximity to one of these lava-spouters, because, while technically active, the volcano had not had a sizable eruption since 1884, and that one had been the first in a century. So the Rangatoa Islanders, a mixture of general Polynesians, some with Chinese blood and others with more than a little Spanish in their background, felt no fear of the "big fella," as they affectionately called the local landmark.

But, it was true, there were some odd stories told about the volcano. One of the Polynesian legends current in these islands told that Wakuaha, a mythical warrior who had been adopted by the gods, had imprisoned beneath Mount Rangatoa an evil fire devil. That was in the beginning of time, of course, and before the stars were made. But fire devils, according to the legends, are hard to kill, and the devil lived on, very angry by now, and weary of the enormous weight of the mountain pressing down upon him. It was his hot, angry breath, panting up the flume, that made that drifting feather of white smoke which gave the island its name. And when, from time to time, the earth trembled a little to some minor subterranean convulsion, that was the fire devil, struggling to free himself.

Someday, the legend concluded, he would succeed in breaking free of restraint. On that unhappy day, the fire devil would come down from the mountain to wreak a terrible vengeance on every living thing. But that was someday, of course; not now.

Tommy Kahua had heard these stories, of course, but he paid them no mind. He did not fear fire devils; in fact, he didn't even believe in them. For Tommy Kahua was an educated young man. He had learned to read (a little) and to write (a little) and even to work with figures (very little) at the Mission school on Huakawki. He was one of the few young men of Rangatoa who had gone to school, and his standing in the small community of Tarapaho had thereby been enhanced. This schooling had been arranged by Señor Felipe Valdez, but not as a charitable gesture. Señor Valdez needed a bright young man to help him run the trading post. This need had become more acute when his only son had been killed by a shark while swimming. Of the local youths, Tommy Kahua had seemed the most eligible. Unfortunately for Señor Valdez, he proved to be one of the laziest, too.

By the time the sun was well up the sky, Tommy had come very close to the top of the mountain. He had checked every trap but one, and all had been empty. He paused here, near the crest, to catch his breath and admire the view. Tree-grown hills rolled away beneath him to the white crescent of the beach, where the lazy Pacific lay rippling in the warm sun. On the other side of the volcano, which rose at the exact center of the island, a bamboo swamp lay, thick and dark. Somewhere along its edge lived "the Yank," an American geologist here to study the mineral deposits.

Looking down at the beach, Tommy saw that his fellow townsmen were astir and about their morning's business. In fact, he saw that a crowd was gathered on the beach about the dock. Something was going on down there, and Tommy strained his sharp eyes to make out what it was. A long, sleek motor launch had pulled up to the wooden dock and strangers were disembarking. One of them was a woman, he saw. From this height and distance, all he could make out was the bright lilac of a summer frock, long legs, and the glimmer of long bright hair. But Tommy grinned. He had an eye for the girls, Tommy did. Especially for blondes.

Tommy was so intent on the strangers arriving below that he did not notice the thing until it was almost upon him.

It was *the smell* that finally dragged his attention away from the sight below.

It was hard to describe, that smell. Hot stone was in it, and burning sulphur. He turned to look—

Here, near the peak, the topsoil had eroded away to naked rock which was actually uncomfortably warm beneath his feet.

A sort of narrow trail was cut through the rock to the crest. Along this path, in the bad old days before the coming of the first white missionaries, Tommy Kahua's ancestors had come at intervals during the year to give the fire devil a bride. The unfortunate young women chosen for this grim honor were first made drunk with date wine, so that their terrified screams would not mar the dignity of the occasion, then bound with ropes of flowers and flung over the brink of the volcano to a mercifully swift death in the seething vapors of the crater.

These sacrifices were made in order to appease the fire devil that Wakuaha had imprisoned below. The theory was, obviously, that if the girls were pretty enough, the demon would be too busy, or too happy, or both, to bother with the destruction of the village. Apparently, it had worked, for, as I have said, the last serious eruption had been in 1884, before Tommy Kahua's father was born.

Up this path Tommy stared, nostrils distended at the hot, sulphurous smell of burnt stone.

The path terminated in a wall of drifting smoke and steam, the base of the snowy plume that floated up against the cobalt sky.

And out of this wall of vapor came lumbering a figure so fantastic and so horrible that Tommy almost fainted at a single glimpse of it.

It was a hideous, squat, wide-shouldered, lump-headed thing, bigger and broader than a man. For some crazy reason, Tommy thought of the illustrations of a troll he had seen in a book of fairy stories back at the Mission school. The thing looked exactly like a troll.

Except that it was covered with molten lava.

Gleaming rivulets of white-hot liquid rock streamed over its mud-colored breast and shoulders and ran dripping down its huge thick ape-like arms, which terminated, he saw, in monstrous paws. Its face, if it possessed one, was hidden from view by a mass of dripping lava.

The molten stone was so hot that it steamed in the air, surrounding the ghastly lumbering monster with clouds of vapor.

Tommy turned as pale as his olive complexion allowed. His eyes rolled back into his head until only the whites showed. He shook all over—arms, legs, head, hands—like a very old man with Parkinson's disease.

Then he began to run.

But before he began to run, he screamed. Once only. But once was enough. That scream ripped his throat lining, it was so loud. And it was so loud that even the people gathered on the beach heard it, a horrible wailing cry drifting down from above. A cry with so much fear in it that the men and women of Tarapaho froze in their tracks, and more than a few crossed themselves at the sound of it.

It was like the screech a damned soul might give voice to, burning in hell.

The cry had come from the mountain, of course. That was plainly obvious; for it had come from above their heads.

The men began to run in the direction from which the awful cry had sounded. Some of them stopped to snatch up barbed fishing spears or the ornately-carven ceremonial stone clubs that had belonged to their ancestors. They were purely ornamental, those clubs. But you could brain a bull with them.

Before long, they got to Tommy Kahua. But someone . . . or something . . . had gotten to him first. Gotten to him and seized him from behind, in a thick-fingered grip the size of a baseball mitt, a grip so fiery-hot that it had seared him to the bone. The mark of that monster paw was burnt into the crisp, blackened flesh like the mark of a huge, hand-shaped branding-iron heated red-hot.

Tommy was dying from shock, first-degree burns, and loss of blood. But he still had a little breath in him.

"The . . . burning troll," he gasped faintly. The men looked at one another, fear naked in their eyes. They knew the legends of this mountain.

"Like a burning troll," he breathed. "Lava running down all over him . . ."

Señor Valdez was kneeling next to the body of poor Tommy Kahua. His face was pale, tense, anxious, and tears stood in his brown eyes.

"Tommy," he said in a broken voice, "Tommy, who did this to you—*who?*"

"The fire devil," said Tommy in a clear, strong voice. Then he lay back on the warm rock and was dead.

Señor Valdez took a red bandanna handkerchief out of

the hip pocket of his white duck trousers, unfolded it, and spread it so that it hid the face of Tommy Kahua.

He directed two of the biggest and strongest of the men to pick up the body and carry it down the mountain. The men nodded and stooped to do so. Then they froze, staring.

A few patches of earth clung to the bare rock, here and there. Thin, scruffy grass grew on one such bit of soil, very near where Tommy Kahua had fallen. Amidst this hummock of grass a *footprint* could clearly be seen. It could be seen so clearly because the heat of it had blackened the grass to soot, and because small flames smoldered and flickered in the grass that stood around the edges of the print.

It was like a man's footprint, but larger. More like that of a bear or of a great gorilla. It had no toes, just one flat, broad pad. And it had seared the grass like red-hot iron.

The men raised their frightened eyes and looked up the slope.

Other prints could be seen, soot-black smudges against bare brown rock.

One set of prints came shambling down the slope from the mouth of the crater to where Tommy had been when the thing, whatever it was, had grabbed him and had killed him with the heat of its burning paws. The second set of prints ascended the slope and vanished over the lip of the crater, where the hot vapor flew.

Dribbles of molten lava were splattered in a trail matching the black paw-prints. The lava was only yellow-hot by now, having cooled a little.

Something monstrous and incredible and alive had come through the boiling vapor, come out of the furnace-heat of that crater. Tommy had seen it, and screamed, and it had killed him by laying its burning paws upon him. Then it had lumbered back up the slope and vanished into the boiling cauldron of the crater again.

The men looked at one another, but said nothing.

There was nothing to say, really.

On their way back down the mountain with Tommy Kahua's body, one of the men turned to Señor Valdez.

"What shall we do?" he asked worriedly. "The police—"

"Can do nothing against a monster, a fire devil," said Señor Valdez firmly, shaking his head.

"What then?"

Señor Valdez rubbed one hand across his brow thoughtfully. When he took away his hand, his eyes shone with determination.

"In my house I have a copy of the latest issue of a magazine," he said. "The name of that magazine is *Na-tion-al Geo-graph-ic.* In the magazine there is an article about a man who helps people. He is a wise man, and a good man, of great wealth and power. He travels all over the world fighting evil-doers and helping people who are in trouble. In one of the little countries in South America, just recently, this man and his assistants helped the poor Indians who were in terror of a man-killing monster. While he was in their country, fighting to destroy this monster, he made a remarkable discovery. He found an ancient city of the Mayas, lost in the jungles for many ages, yet still inhabited by the descendants of the ancient Mayas. He published a report on the spoken Mayan language, as still used by their living descendants, which solved the mystery of how this forgotten language was pronounced. For this he has just been given the Nobel Prize of many dollars. This money he donated to the government of the South American country, so that they might build hospitals, libraries, and schools."

Señor Valdez drew a long breath.

"His name is Prince Zarkon. He lives in Knickerbocker City. I am going to call him on the radio. Perhaps he will come to help us."

"Perhaps so," murmured the man at his side, impressed but yet skeptical. "But why should he? There must be many people who need his aid. Why should he come here?"

"Because I will pay him very much money to do so," replied Señor Valdez. "He can build hospitals and schools with that money, if so he wishes. But I will offer him much, for am I not a man of wealth?"

"You are," admitted the other man, "the richest man on the whole island of Rangatoa."

"It is so!" Señor Valdez smiled with complacent pride. "In the great bank at Mantilla I have a bank account. In it for twenty years I have deposited my money. It was to go for the education of my children, that money, but alas, only one son was given to me, and now God has taken him. So I will pay all of this money to the Prince Zarkon if he will help us. There is *seven hundred and thirty-nine dollars* in the bank at Mantilla in my name!"

"So much! *Madre dios,*" marveled the other.

"Even so much," said Señor Valdez, with pride. "So, you see, my friend, surely the Prince Zarkon will come to help us. At least I will call him on the radio and ask it. Can he say no?"

Together they went down the mountain and into the village, carrying the dead man who was the fire devil's first victim in many centuries.

But not his last!

CHAPTER 2

The Nonplussing of Doc

The radio message that Señor Valdez broadcast from the island of Rangatoa in the Pacific was received by sensitive instruments located within one of the brownstone tenement buildings on a block on the Upper West Side of Knickerbocker City, halfway around the world.

To the eye, this block looked in no way particularly different from any of the hundreds of such to be found in the older residential neighbors of the giant metropolis. Battered ashcans were piled between flights of front steps; lace-curtained windows gazed out on a street where dogs were being walked and children played noisily; rooftops bristled with TV antennae and chimneys; geraniums bloomed in window-boxes; cars were parked at random along the curb. At the end of the block flowed the dark waters of the Henry Hudson River, amidst which a small, tree-grown isle could be glimpsed; beyond rose the palisades of New Jersey.

A closer look would have, perchance, revealed that none of the windows on this block could be seen into: shades were drawn or heavy drapes discreetly closed. And by one of the doors a small, unobtrusively-placed brass plate might have caught the eye. It bore no name or legend, but a single letter in the ancient Greek alphabet: *omega.*

Only a few high city officials and Federal officers knew that, in actuality, this entire block of buildings was a system of false fronts concealing an immense structure built like a fortress, generating its own power and breathing its own carefully recycled air. The innocent-seeming, ordinary-looking facade hid walls of battleship steel, braced and reinforced to resist anything this side of a rampaging tank. And the windows were of heavy, bullet-proof plastic, optically ground to resemble ordinary plate-glass, but tough enough to stand up to anything smaller than a bazooka shell.

For this building housed the Omega group, the most secret and powerful private crime-fighting organization in the world. Behind these fortress walls were the apartments where lived the five Omega men and their master. Herein, as well, were advanced laboratories and machine shops; a fully-equipped hospital facility; storerooms and research libraries; a basement garage housing a fleet of powerful, bullet-proof vehicles of every type and description; a communications center so sophisticated that it could instantly place the Omega men in touch with every foreign capital; computers, Weissmann projectors, telegraphy equipment, a private rooftop observatory; and sealed, fireproof vaults containing a host of ingenious instruments and scientific marvels whose very existence was unsuspected by the outside world.

Beneath folding rooftop bays, a sleek helicopter of advanced design stood fueled and ready to whisk the Omega men to a private airfield located on the island in the river, where hangar facilities were hidden behind clever camouflage which protected them from scrutiny. In one of the upper rooms stood ranked file cabinets containing detailed dossiers on over thirty thousand known international criminals, and automatic radio equipment which monitored and recorded police calls in forty major cities.

Such, then, was Omega—the unsleeping sentinel of liberty, the unrelenting foe of supercrime, the tireless champion of law and order.

It was late afternoon in Knickerbocker City when the call for help was received from the distant Luzon islands. The five Omega men and Chandra Lal, their servant, had gathered in the study upon the instructions of their leader, whom they expected momentarily.

The study was luxuriously appointed with every appurtenance that exquisite taste and unlimited wealth could afford. Thousands of volumes marched in rows on mahogany bookshelves lining the walls; priceless Flemish tapestries glowed in the corners; superb oils by Matisse, Corot, Gaughan, and other masters gleamed in expensive gold frames, while a rare Persian carpet spread its gorgeous colors underfoot. A fresh-laid fire crackled on the grate of an ornate fireplace of Florentine marble, it being a raw, blustery spring day.

Standing before the fire, two men, strikingly dissimilar in every detail of their appearance and background, stood rubbing their hands before the blaze, exchanging a rapidfire verbal duel of insults. One of these was a lanky, sallow-faced, long-legged gentleman of theatrical manner and Italian extraction, with a waxed goatee, satanic mustachios, and lustrous blue-black hair. This was Nick Naldini, former vaudevillian stage magician, escape artist, and reformed con-man and gambler. He had a long-jawed, sardonic face and lazy, amused black eyes, and looked rather like the actor John Carradine gotten up to impersonate Count Dracula. His lounge suit was in impeccable taste, but the total effect was marred by a red velvet smoking jacket and a gaudily-colored silk scarf about his throat.

The man beside him, whose fiery, curled thatch barely reached the magician's bony shoulders, was a husky little bantamweight Irishman with a snub nose and blue eyes, who wore tan slacks and a turtleneck sweater of shamrock-green. This former boxer, and judo and karate expert, was Aloysius Murphy Muldoon, called "Scorchy" by his comrades in peril, the sobriquet having been bestowed upon the feisty little redhead by an admiring sports reporter, in obvious allusion to the speed of his flying fists, which fairly "scorched" the air.

The running feud between these two was of long duration but meant little, for they were actually the firmest and closest of friends, although either would have gone to the stake rather than admit to the fondness and affection each felt for the other.

Seated on the two couches which faced the fire were three other men of unusual appearance. One, a clumsy, lumbering oaf of a man with a slab-sided, dull-eyed face and lank hair of nondescript color, who sat moodily cracking the knuckles of his overgrown paws, looked like a shambling halfwit. Actually, he possessed one of the most remarkable intellects in the world, having been born one of those rare individuals with an eidetic memory, able to remember every fact or figure they have ever read, every face they have ever seen, every voice they have ever heard. This man, Theophilus "Doc" Jenkins, had put his camera eyes, tape-recorder ears, and computer brain to the service of Omega and its mysterious master.

Beside the big, pale-faced oaf with the miraculous mind sat a tanned, handsome, athletic young man whose guileless features and trim physique caused feminine hearts to flutter on five continents—for he had never visited Antarctica. This was Francis "Ace" Harrigan, former crack test-pilot and a famous air ace who had downed forty enemy planes over Indo-China.

Next to him sat a frail, waspish little man with a starved, peevish face and scrawny arms. This skinny little scarecrow was a brilliant scientific genius named Mendel Lowell Parker, an electronic wizard deemed the peer of Tesla and Marconi, whose first two names, as well as his Edison-like brain, had earned him the nickname of "Menlo" Parker, in jesting tribute to Edison himself, the "wizard of Menlo Park." A confirmed bachelor with a furious temper, Menlo could never decide whether he disliked women more than he disliked his nickname, or the other way around.

These three were listening—with varying degrees of amusement, boredom, and exasperation—to the exchange of wise-cracks and insults that was going on between Nick Naldini and Scorchy Muldoon.

"Say, pint-size, it just occurred to me—you could probably make a few bucks renting chest space on that vile-colored sweater of yours to the Irish Tourist Office for a small advertisement," Nick was drawling in his hoarse, whiskey voice. "It would have to be mighty small, I guess, due to the size of the billboard."

Scorchy, who had donned the shamrock-hued garment expressly to annoy his crony, who affected a violent distaste for the verdant color, which (he said, with small, fastidious shudders) always reminded him of Muldoon's Hibernian ancestry, flushed at this crack. Bristling, he balled hard fists as if about to wade into a brawl, which was his second-favorite form of idle amusement, his first being the baiting of Naldini.

"Why, you fugitive from a Mandrake the Magician look-alike contest, another crack about me height and I'll be after showin' yez I kin take on a skinny beanpole wid one fist tied behoind me back!" the ex-boxer snarled, lapsing into his brogue as he generally did whenever his dander was up.

As for Nick Naldini, the lanky stage magician merely smiled.

"A contest between us, my pigmy pugilist," he drawled laconically, "would be contrary to the Marquis of Queensbury rules."

Scorchy scowled. "Hozzat, long, lean, an' larcenous?"

"Due to a certain deficiency in your sum total of inches, you would perforce be hitting me below the belt," smirked the magician with a twinkle in his eye.

"Why, you broken-down third-rate Houdini, Oi'll be after stranglin' yez on yer own chin whiskers, y' long-legged galoot! Lemme at 'im, fellas—"

Chuckling, Nick ducked behind a table, fending off the furious little fighter.

Just then a tall, swarthy Hindu, his head wrapped in an immaculate turban, quietly entered the room, bearing a tray on which cups and a coffeepot were arranged.

"Hey, Chandra Lal," Ace Harrigan spoke up, happy to derail the current direction of the conversation, "you know when the chief is coming up?"

The tall Hindu shook his head, setting the tray down on the coffee table. "The *sahib* has been engaged since early morning with his latest experiments," said the Rajput deferentially. "It is not for Chandra Lal to say when he will be finished."

The five Omega men accepted the cups which the Hindu filled with steaming brown fluid, and sipped with lip-smacking gusto. Until the Indian manservant had joined them a little while ago, they had reluctantly endured Scorchy Muldoon's cooking. The peppery little Irishman fancied himself a gourmet chef, but the actuality was that he couldn't even boil water without ruining its taste. Engaged in drinking the delicious beverage, none of them noticed as a section of bookshelves opened smoothly in the wall to reveal a hidden elevator which connected the big study with the underground laboratory and suite of rooms occupied by their master, who now entered and stood for a moment, observing them.

The man who had just entered the room from his secret sanctum beneath street level seemed at first glance an ordinary-looking personage. His height was an inch or two over six feet, which meant that he was dwarfed by the towering hugeness of Doc Jenkins, and his physical development was so trim and perfectly symmetrical that he looked slender enough, in comparison to the brawny build of Scorchy Muldoon. It was only at second or at third glance that you began to notice the unusual details of his appearance.

His complexion was a strange, tawny shade suggesting the presence of Oriental blood. His features were of classic perfection, literally as handsome as those of a Greek god—in point of fact, his visage bore a startling resemblance to the features of the marble Perseus of Canova, if not indeed to the Apollo Belvedere itself. Had his superbly regular features not possessed an impassive and majestic calm, they might have suggested effeminacy in their striking beauty. But his eyes, large, deep-set, wide-apart, and of black magnetic fire hinted at the force of character and strength of will and powerfully masculine maturity this seemingly-young man concealed within him.

His perfectly-proportioned figure was dressed in a turtleneck pullover made of stretch fabric in gunmetal gray. Gray, too, was the supple suede jacket and close-fitting slacks he wore, and his suede shoes with rubber soles were of the identical hue, which, for some reason, he usually affected. His sleek head of hair was of the precise shade of gray as his clothing and was arranged in meticulous locks across his brow in a fashion curiously similar to the antique Roman portrait busts in the International Museum of Art on the east side of Central Park.

His brow was spacious, noble, high, denoting an intelligence many times superior to that of the ordinary man. In truth he was not in any sense of the word ordinary: out of nowhere he had appeared, some ten years earlier, in the small Balkan country of Novenia, whose strategic importance was fully recognized both by the Western and by the Eastern powers, due to its control of the only known source of the rare metal rhombium, vital to the generation of nuclear power and the manufacture of atomic weapons. He had introduced easy, inexpensive methods of processing rhombium, overnight transforming the troubled little country into a wealthy and powerful nation whose grateful populace, reviving the ancient regalia of an extinct house, had made him their monarch. Before abdicating the throne in favor of the model democracy he swiftly established, he had written a new constitution now recognized as one of the noblest and most civilized of democratic charters penned since the American Constitution itself. Retiring to self-exile in the United States, under the diplomatic immunity granted with full Congressional approval to him as a respected former head of state, he had registered his patents on the rhombium process which today had made him one of the wealthiest private citizens on earth. This immense fortune he dedicated, as he had dedicated the remainder of his life, to a secret war against those super-criminals who used the wizardry of advanced scientific technology to gain a hold on the superstitious fears of common men.

For he was, in actuality, a time-traveler from the remote future, come back from a distant age nearly destroyed by aeons of criminal misrule to change mankind's grim future by altering its past. There he had been Arkon Z-1000, the final result in an age-long program of genetic engineering designed to produce a superman strong and wise enough to wage battle against the criminal masterminds who had arisen during the closing decades of the Twentieth Century and who had ruled for generations a neo-feudal world which they, in their callous greed, had plunged into a Dark Age of appalling internecine strife from which his own future had slowly emerged to shelter the surviving remnants of mankind and to preserve the awesome scientific wisdom salvaged from a ruined past.

Such was Prince Zarkon of Novenia—Lord of the Unknown, Man of Mysteries, Nemesis of Evil!

In a few terse, well-chosen words, Prince Zarkon apprised his lieutenants of the radio message his sensitive instruments had picked up from the island of Rangatoa. The events surrounding the mysterious death of Tommy Kahua, and the old legend of the fire devil supposedly imprisoned underneath the volcanic mountain, were swiftly told. Scorchy was impressed by the story.

"Cripes, chief! A monster that crawls out o' the crater o' a live volcano, drippin' all over wid molten lava, an' kills folks with a touch o' his burnin' paws! *Wow!* Sure sounds like our sort o' case, all right."

"Exactly my own thought, Scorchy," said Zarkon quietly.

"How we gonna get there, though, chief?" asked Ace Harrigan thoughtfully. "Too far away for the *Shooting*

Star to be much use," he mused, referring to Omega's private jet, one of the fastest in the world. "Maybe we better take the big bird. . . ."

Zarkon agreed. In a private airfield on Long Island the Omega men kept their big, long-distance transport plane, the *Skyrocket*. Only this huge craft could carry the five of them, together with the clothing and equipment they would need to carry with them, to the other side of the planet.

They discussed ways and means, selecting the cases of equipment they thought it likely they would require on this adventure. During this exchange, Doc Jenkins maintained a glum silence.

"Hey, Doc," Scorchy spoke up suddenly, "what d'ya know about this-here island, Rangatoa, anyway? Unlimber that magic noodle of yours; we better know what we're gettin' into."

The big, pale-skinned man said nothing. He looked distinctly unhappy and forlorn. Finally, in a grudging voice, he said that Rangatoa was one of the smaller islands of the Luzon group, the latitude and longitude of which he rattled off in his usual way. Then he informed them that the islands, which had formerly been a colony of Spain, had been granted their independence by the League of Nations in 1930 and had formed the Luzon Union under the active encouragement of Juan Mindoro, the world-known Luzon millionaire, philanthropist, and patriot.

"—The center of the Union is the island of Luzon itself, comprising some seven hundred and thirty-two square miles. The capital city is Mantilla, situated on Mantilla Bay, and a center of shipping in the Pacific. The principal products of the Luzon islands are tea, copra, teakwood, bamboo, manganese—"

"Yeah, yeah, that's swell," interrupted Scorchy hastily. "But what about Rangatoa itself?"

The big man's face became even more glum, solemn, and lugubrious than before. He said nothing. Suddenly Scorchy's Killarney-blue eyes lit up with wicked glee, and he burst out laughing. The others stared at him puzzledly.

"Don't you guys get it?" crowed the pint-sized boxer. "Big brain, over there, *just plain don't know nothing about Rangatoa!*"

The woeful expression on Doc's heavy face confirmed this unlikely fact. The Omega lieutenants exchanged glances of amazement. It was literally unheard of for the big man with the eidetic memory not to be an inexhaustible fountain of facts and figures on any and every conceivable topic. They had never before seen him so nonplussed.

"Goldarnit, Scorchy, the Luzon group's made up of *thousands* of little tiny reefs and atolls and islands . . . ain't nothing special about this one . . . I . . . I just don't have any particular information about Rangatoa, that's all," mumbled Doc Jenkins in a sad voice, crimson with embarrassment.

But Scorchy wasn't listening. He was doubled up with laughter.

CHAPTER 3

At the Cobalt Club

While his lieutenants went about packing their clothing and personal gear, and assembling the big equipment cases they had decided to take with them, Zarkon placed a few local telephone calls, then descended to his basement garage and picked a low-slung, powerful automobile. Driving it up the ramp and through the big, armor-plated, power-driven doors, he emerged onto the street and drove across town to his club which stood on a fashionable, exclusive sidestreet off Fifth Avenue.

Parking at the curb before the imposing marble facade which dated from the turn of the century and had been designed by the famous architect Stanford White, Zarkon entered the lobby and called over the attendant.

"I am supposed to meet Colonel Renwick here, and Admiral Winslow," he said. "Have either of them arrived yet?"

"Yes, Your Highness, Colonel Renwick asked for you only a few minutes ago. I believe you will find the gentleman either in the study or at the bar. Admiral Winslow has not yet arrived, however; when he does, I will tell him that Your Highness is already here."

Nodding his thanks, the Man from Tomorrow entered the study, a large, long room decorated richly but in flawless taste. At this hour of the afternoon it was all but deserted; however, in leather easy chairs drawn up beneath one of the huge windows he recognized two men whom he knew and strolled over to speak with them.

The older man, his silver hair gleaming in the afternoon sunlight, which glinted from the pince-nez glasses affixed to his high-bridged, aristocratic nose, smiled affably as Zarkon approached.

"Ah! A pleasant surprise, my dear Prince. We see you so seldom these days . . . I trust you are acquainted with Benson, here," he said, nodding to the gray-haired man with stiff, colorless, immobile features, who was seated next to him.

"Indeed I do, Philo; how are you, Richard?" nodded Prince Zarkon with a quiet smile.

The white-faced man said through unmoving lips, "Well enough, sir. Nice to see you again. I was just remarking to Vance here that the club seems deserted today. Usually you will find Cranston or Wentworth lounging in a corner, but today the place is empty."

"I believe Cranston is still in San Francisco," murmured Zarkon. "I was supposed to meet Colonel Renwick here. Have either of you seen him?"

Vance nodded, his pince-nez gleaming. "One of Savage's team, isn't he? The engineer? He looked in a moment ago; you will probably find him in the bar."

Zarkon made his thanks and entered the bar, a low-ceilinged room, cozy and dark, with a huge fireplace at one end and old oil portraits of former members along the walls above the tables. There he spied the man he had come to consult, chatting with a tall, well-dressed man with gray-shot temples and smooth, dark hair with whom Zarkon was slightly acquainted. This person was a wealthy man-about-town named Van Loan.

Zarkon strolled up to the bar and introduced himself to Colonel Renwick, nodding to Van Loan.

"Oh, hiya, Prince! Been lookin' all over for ya. Guess I was a little early," boomed the big engineer in a hearty voice, shaking hands.

"It was kind of you to come," smiled Zarkon. "Have you two gentlemen introduced yourselves? Mr. Richard Curtis Van Loan, Colonel John Renwick. Dick, may I order you another of whatever you were drinking?"

Van Loan shook his head with a quiet smile. "Thank you, but no. I was just killing time, waiting for my guest to arrive. I was supposed to have an early dinner with my father's old friend Frank Havens, the newspaper publisher. And here he is now! I'll leave you two gentlemen to your business. It was a pleasure to meet you, Renwick."

"Same here," boomed the big man, shaking hands. As Van Loan left the bar to meet his guest, Zarkon took his stool. Renwick was a huge, cheerful man who topped Zarkon by some two inches and outweighed him by at least fifty pounds of bone and beef. He had a tanned, weather-beaten face under a tousled shock of gray hair, and the most enormous pair of hands you could find for twenty states around. They were ham-sized mitts of solid gristle, big enough to fit quart buckets. This feature, and the fact that while his voice was cheerful his face wore an expression of permanent and abiding gloom, made him stick out in a crowd, whose members probably would not have recognized him for the famous adventurer, traveler, and civil engineer he was. Dams, railways, tunnels, and bridges the world over bore his name, however.

"Howja know I was in town, anyway?" he asked cheerfully, after a long guzzle into his martini glass. "I been retired for years, y'know; got me a big ranch out in Wyoming now, an' hardly ever get t' town."

"Yes, I know." Zarkon smiled. "But your friend Brooks once mentioned the fact that you and your former colleagues still get together for an annual reunion dinner whose date, I believe, is tomorrow."

"Holy Cow, you hit it on th' nose!" boomed the glum-faced giant happily. "Betcha don't know why that particular date, though!"

"Yes, I do," said Zarkon with a rare chuckle. "It marks the occasion, back in 1918, when you first met your friends. You were all prisoners of war together in a German camp, the Loki *stalag,* near the end of the First World War. . . ."

"Holy Cow," rumbled the big engineer. "Sounds like ol' Ham's been shooting off his mouth! I better tell him t' hush up before he gives away all our secrets! Say, what'd'ja wanna see me about, anyway, Prince?"

"Rangatoa Island in the Luzon group," said Zarkon. "Weren't you out there recently on a mining survey?"

"Sure was," boomed Renwick, lighting up a big cigar. "Retired or not, they sometimes coax me off th' ranch by danglin' enough money under my nose! Big minin' outfit wanted a survey of them islands t' see if there was anything out there worth a big operation. Nothin' on Rangatoa, though, but some baxterite deposits; an' not enough baxterite to get excited about, either. Found some decent manganese lodes on couple o' the bigger islands, but th' company decided not to dig. See, you'd hafta deepen th' channels between them islands to get the big ore-ships in, and that'd cost ya more'n th' metals'd be worth."

"I see," nodded Zarkon. "What was the name of the firm that hired you to perform the survey?"

"Outfit called Pacific Mining and Minerals," answered Renwick. "Guy in charge is a comical geezer name of Braxton T. Crawley. They got an office in San Francisco, another in Honolulu, and a small one in Mantilla. Not much out in the Luzons, y'know; mostly igneous rock out there—islands are volcanic in origin."

Glancing at his watch, the big man tossed down the rest of his drink. "Say, I gotta be gettin' along now, Prince, if that's all I can tell ya."

A tall man with military posture and dignified gray temples entered the bar shortly after this. Spotting Zarkon, he strode over and introduced himself and they shook hands. Rear Admiral Donald A. Winslow, now retired, declined Zarkon's offer of a drink, suggesting coffee instead. They went into the study and took chairs by the window where Vance and Benson had sat earlier, and Zarkon summoned an attendant, ordering coffee for two. Then he wasted no time in broaching the subject of his interest.

"Weren't you in the Pacific during the war, Admiral?" he inquired. "I seem to recall that you were engaged in the battle off Mantilla Bay. I'm particularly interested in a small island to the south, called Rangatoa; any first-hand information you can tell me about the place would be appreciated."

Don Winslow sipped his coffee thoughtfully. "I had command of the *Exeter* during that engagement, yes," he said. "And, now that you mention it, at one point we were moored off an island named Rangatoa. I recall sending some parties ashore for reconnaissance, just to be sure we didn't have any of the enemy holed up there." With brisk, well-chosen words, the Admiral related what he knew of the island, which was mostly negative; that is, outside of a small village composed mainly of native fishermen with a sprinkling of individuals of mixed Spanish descent, there was nothing at all on the island, save for the jungles, a stretch of swamp, and the volcanic mountain itself, which dominated the entire central portion of the tiny isle. There were no other villages or settlements and never had been.

Zarkon asked a number of questions, few of which Admiral Winslow was able to answer with any certainty or in any sort of concrete detail. Realizing that he wasn't being of much help, the Admiral shrugged self-deprecatingly, and apologized.

"I'm afraid I'm not being very useful to you, Prince Zarkon," he grinned. "The fact of the matter is, there simply isn't anything on Rangatoa that is of any real interest to anybody; few people live there, and not much of importance has ever happened there; at least, nothing that I know about."

"That's quite all right," Zarkon said. "You've been of help, actually: just knowing there's nothing much there is to have learned something about the place. Everything I can find out concerning Rangatoa may come in handy. We're going out there soon, and I have always found that it comes in handy to learn as much as possible about a certain locale before visiting it. But I want to make certain of one thing before I let you go. It is a definite fact that you discovered no secret Japanese installations on the island? No underground bunkers or gun-emplacements or storage facilities? No hidden base of any kind?"

"None whatsoever," said Winslow in a positive tone. "The soil, I remember, was of very hard-packed clay over solid rock. It would have been tremendously difficult to have hollowed out any installations underground. And the islanders themselves assured us at the time that no Japanese landings had ever been made on the island."

Leaving the Cobalt Club, Zarkon called his lieutenants on the mobile radiophone unit with which his car was equipped, learning that, as he had instructed, they had already made the trip to the secret airbase on Long Island and were loading up the plane. Chandra Lal had packed Prince Zarkon's gear and belongings for him and they were already on the aircraft. So the Prince, instead of returning to Omega headquarters, drove across one of the midtown bridges to the island and headed for the airfield where his men awaited him.

Most of the planes used by Omega were stored on the little island in the middle of the river. There also the Omega men moored their seagoing craft, which included a powerful luxury yacht which had the firepower of a pocket battleship, although you would never have suspected it from a look at the superbly designed craft, and an atomic submarine, the *Captain Nemo*, which was believed to be the world's only privately owned submersible thus powered with nuclear engines.

But the big, long-distance plane needed more of a runway than the limited size of Omega Island could afford; hence, the necessity of a land-based airfield. Since the Omega organization, insofar as it was possible to do so, concealed all details of its operations from the public, to insure its safety from the cunning criminals who were the enemies against which Omega had been created as opposition, the location and purpose of the airbase had to be kept secret.

The field itself, which was located in a largely uninhabited part of Long Island, had been built back in the 1930s by a wealthy, adventure-loving, energetic businesswoman who had parlayed her exclusive Park Avenue beauty salon—Patricia, Incorporated—into a multimillion-dollar business. Liking the idea of a private airfield, she built one, disguising the fact with signs which falsely identified the place as the "Norpen Lumber Company." When she married and sold her beauty salon, she was easily persuaded to sell the private airfield as well, which Zarkon had purchased as a home for the *Skyrocket*. The experimental superplane was then being constructed, according to Zarkon's design, by the Hazzard Laboratories out on College Point, Long Island, the same firm which had built his special helicopter, the *Silver Ghost*, to his own specifications.

The ride out to the so-called Norpen Lumber Company was dull and uneventful. So Zarkon decided to let the big car drive itself while he mentally reviewed the data which had thus far been gathered on the island of Rangatoa. Perhaps I should explain here that the big limousine Zarkon was using for this trip was another one of his experimental vehicles, called *Greyhound*. The powerful car packed underneath its hood a super-miniaturized radar guidance system, robot pilot, and traffic computer, hooked up together in such a way that *Greyhound* could scan the highway with its electronic senses and drive itself automatically.

The miracle automobile, however, usually could not cope with the tangled traffic of Knickerbocker City's busy streets. Even a computer, Zarkon learned ruefully, was unable to figure out how to negotiate the metropolitan rush-hour traffic. Here, on a lonely stretch of Long Island highway, on the other hand, *Greyhound*'s "robot-chauffeur" functioned perfectly.

Turning off the highway at the Norpen Lumber Company sign, the sleek gray limousine followed a dirt road through thick stands of trees carefully situated to block all views of the secret airbase. At this point Zarkon shut off the computer and regained manual control of the auto.

He found his men all set and ready to go. Sunset flamed

red beyond the trees which concealed the hills to the west, but the field was brilliantly, if unobtrusively, lit by ground-level banks of floodlights which would turn themselves off automatically, once the great rocketplane had cleared the end of the runway.

Parking *Greyhound* in one of the seemingly-dilapidated outbuildings, whose rusty walls of flimsy-looking corrugated iron concealed walls as thick as those of a bank-vault, he joined his friends on the field.

"All packed up and fueled and ready to go, chief," grinned Ace Harrigan. The famous aviator, naturally, would serve as their pilot during the flight, although any of the others could spell him at the controls if needed. They were all expert pilots and were equally adept behind the wheel of every other kind of vehicle, except for Scorchy Muldoon. That is to say, the peppery little redhead could fly a plane or maneuver a boat with the best of them, but when it came to cars, the feisty bantamweight was about as useless as a polar bear in the Sahara, and as much out of his domain. It was a standing joke among Prince Zarkon's lieutenants that Scorchy couldn't drive a car for more than thirty yards without running into something—even if he had to climb up on the sidewalk in order to find something to hit.

The Irishman fiercely resented their jokes on this topic. Privately, he considered himself a born driver: to his way of thinking, all of the automobiles in the world were leagued together in a secret mechanical conspiracy to make him look like a half-blind fumble-fingers whenever he got behind the wheel of one of them. It was, therefore, Scorchy's way to insist on driving a car at every possible opportunity—to the considerable endangerment of any pedestrians in the neighborhood, and to the detriment of every traffic regulation ever devised by the city fathers in all their wisdom. The pint-sized prize-fighter figured stubbornly that it was only a matter of time before the automobiles of the world relented in their plot to make him look bad. This had yet to occur.

Entering the *Skyrocket*, the Omega men chose seats in the rear while Ace went forward into the cabin. A few moments later the jet engines, which powered the craft during takeoff and landing, woke to coughing life. The sleek fuselage pointed down the illuminated runway; the fabric quivered to the throbbing impulse of the engines; slowly, at first, then with increasing speed, the experimental craft hurtled down the lane of lights and lifted gently into the sky. The brightly-lit field vanished below. The plane ascended until it had reached the height of thirty-seven thousand feet, at which altitude it leveled off.

Then the mighty rocket engines awoke. These tubes thrust from the tail assembly of the aircraft and could generate a truly fantastic velocity, far surpassing that of a conventional jet. Using a special hyper-condensed fuel of Zarkon's own formula, the rockets could drive the big bird around the world and back without refueling. It would take them to the central Pacific in a little over six hours.

CHAPTER 4

Damsel in Distress

Just before Tommy Kahua had met his grisly end under the burning paws of the fire devil, he had glimpsed from his vantage-point at the crest of the volcanic mountain the arrival of a motor launch bearing a young woman. He was destined never to learn who she was, nor her role in the sequence of uncanny events which had its beginning in his death.

Had he looked a bit farther out to sea, however, he would have been able to recognize the trim white hull of a luxurious yacht moored at anchor off the reef. This was the yacht *Phoenicia,* out of Honolulu and San Francisco; it belonged to the young lady with the long slim legs and long bright hair and dainty lilac frock whom he had seen getting out of the launch.

As it happened, Miss Phoenicia Mulligan had never before visited the island of Rangatoa, and might not be doing so now had it not been that six months had passed since she had last seen her fiancé. When you are young and in love, to be separated for six months is like being apart for six years. And since it seemed likely that her boy-friend would be remaining on the island for another six months, if his infrequent letters were any indication, the impatient young lady had decided to seize the bull by the horns and visit him.

When she got out of the launch and onto the wooden dock, the citizens of the little village of Tarapaho were too excited over the mysterious tragedy that had befallen poor Tommy Kahua to pay much attention to their visitor. The two sailors who had driven the launch ashore were thus obliged to carry her bags to the foot of the main (and only) street of Tarapaho, while she followed, looking plaintively around for someone to direct her to the man she had come so far to meet.

Most of the menfolk of the tribe had gone up the mountain to find and bring back the body of Tommy Kahua. Only the women and children were left. Many of the younger women of Tarapaho eyed the expensive gown and fashionably coiffured blond hair of Miss Phoenicia Mulligan with interest bordering on fascination. She, in turn, looked them over with curious eyes. Most of them were slim and willowy, with dark flashing eyes, full lips, and long rippling black hair. They were, most of them, knockouts: the sort of girls who could easily have caused a traffic jam back in San Francisco.

Now, as it happened, Phoenicia Mulligan herself had caused more than a few traffic jams on Market Street. Which goes to suggest that the blond girl was something of a contender in the knockout class, too. This was undeniably so. In fact, several score of the more eligible and handsome bachelors in San Francisco and Honolulu society, if queried on the subject, would gladly have filed affidavits to that effect, Miss Phoenicia Mulligan was a four-alarm whangdoozle, even when stacked against the dark-eyed maidens of Rangatoa.

But there is just no accounting for taste. And it had, in fact, occurred on more than one occasion to Phoenicia

Mulligan that the reason for her boy-friend's extended stay on the island might be centered in one such sarong-clad bit of femininity. Just in case this was the case, Phoenicia had deliberately failed to apprise her fiancé of her impending arrival on the island. Hence, she had only herself to blame that the young man was not now waiting at the foot of the dock to greet her.

When the men of the village came trooping back with the body of Tommy Kahua, the duties of island hospitality took precedence over the formalities. Señor Valdez, as the foremost citizen of the little settlement, hastened to pay his respects to the blond heiress, whom he recognized as the niece and ward of Braxton T. Crawley, head of the firm of Pacific Mining & Minerals. Señor Valdez had never met nor even seen Miss Mulligan before, but her name and picture very frequently adorned the social columns of the Honolulu newspaper to which he subscribed.

"How do you do, Señor Valdez." The girl smiled. "I'm here to visit the PM and M survey engineer, my fiancé, Mr. John James Jones—"

The store-owner wrinkled his high brow at this unfamiliar name. But then his expression cleared. "Of course!" he exclaimed with a smile. "The señorita has reference to the young gentleman we of the island know as 'the Yankee.' But, it is to be regretted, the young man is not here. Indeed, we have seen nothing of him for some weeks now."

"But I thought John was staying here," Phoenicia protested.

"Here on the island, yes," nodded Señor Valdez. "But not here in the village. The young man has a place on the other side of the island, on the edge of the swamp—"

"A house, you mean?"

Señor Valdez shrugged in a deprecating manner. "A—what is the word?—a shack, really. Once, perhaps twice in a month he will come to my small establishment for the purchase of canned foods and coffee and other necessities. But, as I say, we have not had the pleasure of a visit from the gentleman now for some weeks. . . ."

Phoenicia Mulligan had observed the corpse of Tommy Kahua as it was carried into his hut, and she had heard and understood just enough of the excited babble of questions, answers, and exclamations which the excited villagers had voiced, to realize something of the enigma of the young man's death. She was conscious now of a vague prickle of fear and worry and concern.

"Could anything have . . . happened to John?" she asked perturbedly.

Señor Valdez chewed his lip uncertainly. An hour before, he would have given his oath that nothing existed on the island of Rangatoa that was likely to bring a strong, alert, intelligent young man who took reasonably sensible precautions, to a bad end. But Tommy Kahua had been an able young man, certainly smart and athletic enough to take care of himself. So now he could not be as positive as earlier he would have been.

"The señorita will, I feel certain, understand that we must see to the burying of our unfortunate friend; also, the police must be consulted in the matter. Indeed, I have but even now sent a radio message to the mainland, begging assistance from the one man clever and altruistic enough to not only come to our assistance in combating this terrible thing, but in solving the mystery. Hence, we shall be very busy with many things to do. However, I will myself at once dispatch one of my people to the residence of Señor Jones, not only to ascertain the fact of his safety, but to inform him of the delightful surprise of your arrival."

"That is very thoughtful of you," smiled Phoenicia.

"Pray do not mention it! It will be my pleasure. And also I wish to offer the señorita such small comforts as my poor establishment may afford, while you are waiting for the arrival of your intended husband."

Phoenicia indicated that he was very kind. Señor Valdez ordered the young men standing about to escort the señorita to his store and to see that her luggage was disposed according to her wishes. Then he summoned a cheerfully grinning, healthy-looking native boy and sent him into the jungle to the shack where the young geologist was stationed, bidding him waste no time along the way. Then he himself followed the blond girl and the boys who carried her luggage, entered the trading post, and ordered the fat, smiling native woman who cooked and cleaned for him to see to the comfort of their visitor, and to serve tea at the earliest opportunity.

"I did not understand that the Yankee—I mean, Señor Jones—was employed by your uncle's firm," he said later as they had tea on the veranda. "It was my understanding that Señor Jones was conducting a survey on his own recognizance, as it were."

Phoenicia smiled and brushed back a lock of blond hair.

"That's about the way things are, Señor Valdez," the girl explained. "I'm afraid that Uncle Braxton took a dislike to Johnny, for some reason. He called him a 'fortune hunter,' and claimed he was only after me for my money. Fooey on him, the interfering old busybody! Johnny quit the survey team in a huff. He started his own one-man company, and has been going about the islands hoping to make a big find on his own—something that would make him, well, independent, if not exactly rich. Then he planned to come back, beard Uncle Braxton in the lion's den, so to speak, and carry me off in triumph, more or less —having proved he could make his own fortune, instead of marrying me for mine."

Señor Valdez smiled politely and murmured a vague response. It all sounded rather impossibly romantic to him, although he was too much of a gentleman to say so. His own people, he thought, had much more sensible ways of handling such matters. A suitable young man was chosen by the bride's family, and that was that. Money arrangements were settled beforehand, and love, you might say, came later. This seemed to Señor Valdez a most civilized arrangement, far superior to the reckless ways of other races when dealing with such matters.

With nightfall no word had yet come from Mr. John James Jones, nor had the native boy returned with any message. Instead, a contingent of police had arrived from Mantilla in a large motorboat to examine the body of the slain boy and to investigate his murder. Señor Valdez was busy with them, and perforce left Phoenicia more or less to herself.

The girl was beginning to get restless. She had dispatched the motor-launch back to her yacht to fetch more sensible clothes, including waterproof boots for the swampy jungle, and also a gunbelt which contained a loaded revolver and several clips of ammunition. The girl was a crack shot with any variety of firearm, and had taken the ladies' marksmanship medal of the San Francisco Gun Club three years in a row. When her clothes arrived, Phoenicia retired into the guest-room which Señor Valdez had graciously placed at her disposal and swiftly changed into the whipcord breeches, boots, shirt, and safari jacket her men had brought from the yacht.

All this talk about mysterious monsters and uncanny murders had gotten her dander up. Unlike most beautiful young heiresses, Phoenicia Mulligan was no pampered darling of the country club set, but an enterprising young woman with a passion for excitement, a love of adventure, a knack for getting into trouble, and the cool head, steady hand, and intestinal fortitude required for getting *out* of it in one piece. She had hunted lions in the Sahara, scuba-dived for Spanish treasure in the Caribbean, and searched for Mayan ruins in the fever-swamps and viper-infested jungles of Yucatan.

With all that experience, she was not going to just sit here sipping tea on the veranda, while her fiancé was in danger—or missing—or both!

The police from Luzon were thorough and efficient, but could not explain anything. At Señor Valdez' insistence, they climbed to the peak of the mountain and examined the scene of the crime, but found nothing. The blackened footprints of the fire devil, which had still been smoldering when the islanders had reached the site, had continued to smolder until by now they were mere shapeless and blackened patches of scorched grass. The police doctor, who examined the body, could not say for certain that what had seared poor Tommy Kahua to death had been a hand, or even a paw. Privately, he thought the island boy had strayed too close to the lip of the crater for safety, and had burned himself by accident. As for the so-called "footprints," these were dismissed as simply burnt patches of grass, set afire by drifting sparks or flying cinders. Winding up their cursory investigation, the police put the island boy's demise down to death by misadventure, turned his body over to the villagers for burial, returned to their motorboat, and sailed off for the main island.

Señor Valdez shook his head grimly. What more could you expect from the authorities, he thought to himself. Mantilla was a big city. The Mantilla police were accustomed to dealing with the familiar spectrum of urban crimes—car theft, drunken driving, robbery, armed assault. What could they be expected to know of island legends or fire devils?

Night fell. Tommy Kahua was buried in the village plot, with all his friends in attendance. The moon came up, spreading the black sea with liquid silver and frosting the edges of the palms.

And still no word had come as to the whereabouts of John James Jones.

Señor Valdez crossed himself apprehensively, and dispatched another boy around the island to the little swamp-edge shack where the young American geologist lived alone. Before long the second boy returned with frightful news. The shack was deserted and the Yankee was gone. And, what was worse, much worse, the first messenger had been found. He was sprawled face down on the side of the mountain, *dead from a terrible burn like the mark of a gigantic paw, hot as liquid fire.*

Miss Phoenicia Mulligan was terribly upset. She instantly demanded of Señor Valdez that a full-scale search be organized for the missing geologist. Señor Valdez, harried and concerned, protested that they could hardly find anything in the jungle by night, and much less in the swamps, which were tricky enough to negotiate by day. With dawn, he vowed, half the male population of Tarapaho would be out searching for the Yankee.

That was not good enough for Phoenicia Mulligan, although she said nothing and pretended to be satisfied.

She knew that the islanders were frightened, their superstitious fears aroused by the mysterious deaths. But she didn't intend to just sit around all night, waiting for day. Not when the young man she intended to marry was lost or injured or in horrible danger.

Returning to her room, Phoenicia closed and latched the door. Then she climbed out of the window and threaded her way through the plowed fields near the trading post and vanished into the darkness.

It would consume valuable time to circle the perimeter of the island by the safe, sane, and sensible route followed by the two island boys Señor Valdez had sent. A much quicker shortcut would be to climb the mountain, which rose directly behind the trading post, and descend on the other side. There, at the foot of the volcano, she could easily find the shack where John James Jones had been living. Señor Valdez had described its location very precisely. And the tropic moonlight was almost as bright as day. Phoenicia was a plucky girl, capable and determined, and she had climbed mountains before. She didn't think there would be any trouble about climbing this one.

Nor was there, until she had reached the top.

It had been somewhere around here, she knew, that the island boy, Tommy Kahua, had been burned to death by the fiery hands of the mysterious monster. Clenching her revolver and tightening her jaw stubbornly, the blond girl gingerly circled the lip of the crater and started down the other side.

It was hard to see the way. Steam and sulphurous smoke rose from the top of the volcano, and the stiff breeze blowing in from the sea sent these vapors into her eyes, stinging them and blurring her vision with tears.

Then she glimpsed something coming at her through the smoke—

Phoenicia stared unbelievingly at the lumbering thing, which dripped rivulets of molten lava.

Then she lifted her revolver, took quick aim, and fired at it. Again and again she pumped steel-jacketed lead into the flaming ogre, until the revolver was empty.

And then she began to scream.

CHAPTER 5

Fat Man with Mustache

Once the *Skyrocket* had attained its cruising altitude, thirty-seven thousand feet, the experimental craft leveled off. The conventional motors died: the rocket-tubes in the tail assembly coughed into life. A bolt of thundering flame speared from the tubes, thrusting the rocket-plane ahead with terrific velocity. Maintaining its present height of some seven miles above the earth, the *Skyrocket* would travel halfway around the world in a matter of mere hours.

In the heated, sound-proof, heavily-insulated cabin, Zarkon and his lieutenants got down to work. As a rule, before they actually got into one of their adventures the Omega men tried to gather all the information they could assemble which seemed to have a bearing on the present business at hand.

The cabin of the *Skyrocket* was not only comfortable to the point of luxury, but it was fully equipped with radiophones. In rear compartments, ingeniously-miniaturized compartments held workshops, chemical and biological laboratories, a fully-equipped darkroom, an arsenal of sophisticated weapons, and even a complete medical lab and operating room.

But it was the radiophones that the Omega men turned

to now. While Zarkon called the headquarters of the Federal Bureau of Investigation in Washington, inquiring if any of the individuals thus far involved in the matter had criminal records, Doc Jenkins put through a call to the Geographical Society for more detailed information on the island of Rangatoa, including recent seismograph readings.

While these matters were being attended to, Nick Naldini contacted a Wall Street stockbroker friendly to the Omega organization and obtained from him a clean bill of health, financially speaking, on Pacific Mining & Minerals. He learned that the outfit had never been involved in anything shady, and was worth millions. Seated beside him, Scorchy was talking to the police chief in Mantilla. He hung up, having ascertained that Señor Valdez and the other citizens of Rangatoa had no local police records and that Valdez came from an old, long-established family whose history went back to the first Spanish sailors to discover the Luzon islands.

"Anything?" asked Zarkon as Scorchy hung up the receiver.

The little Irishman shook his head gloomily. "Nothin'," he said. "Valdez is clean as clean can be, and nobody on th' island so much as has a parking ticket on his record. Ain't even been a major crime committed on Rangatoa for forty years, and then it was just two lovesick local Lotharios got in a fight over some island colleen, an' one brained t'other with a warclub. How about you? Anythin' from the feds?"

Zarkon indicated that there was not.

Menlo Parker, who had nothing in particular to do, fidgeted edgily. "How's about me, chief?"

"Menlo, you can call the Luzon Ministry of Justice in Mantilla and apprise them of our impending arrival,"

Zarkon instructed. "As we will be bringing firearms and other weapons into their country, to say nothing of explosives, we have to inform them. Give them our Interpol authority and the name and number of our sponsor at the Department of Justice in Washington, if you will. We don't wish to get into any trouble with the local lawmen, who might take exception to our poaching on their preserves, so to speak."

"Right, chief!" beamed Menlo, turning to one of the phones.

"Whatcha got for me t' do next, chief?" inquired Scorchy.

"The headquarters of Pacific Mining and Minerals is in San Francisco, I believe," Zarkon murmured. "It might be a good idea for you to speak with them. I want to see the minerals survey report for Rangatoa, and the name of the man who signed it. They can send this over the photofax equipment. I suggest you go directly to the top with this request. The president of the company is a Mr. Braxton T. Crawley. If he isn't in, ask where you can call him."

"You got it, chief," grinned the Pride of the Muldoons. A little while later he detached himself from the earphones long enough to report that Braxton T. Crawley was himself in the Luzon islands, having flown from the San Francisco airport the day before.

"Seems this Crawley character has a niece always running off to go deep-sea fishing, or lion-hunting on safari, or archaeological digs in Mexico, that sort of thing. Always ends up gettin' into trouble," grinned Scorchy. "This time the gal has sneaked off in her yacht to meet her boy-friend in the Luzons."

"Where in the Luzons?"

Scorchy shrugged. "Dunno. This here boy-friend—he's a guy name of John James Jones, by the way—used to work for PM and M but got chased off by his gal's guardian. That's Crawley; the guardian, I mean. The boyfriend's out to make a fortune somewhere on his own, so that this Crawley character can't cuss him out for bein' a fortune-hunter! This here John James Jones took off in a huff months ago and hasn't been heard of since, leastways not that Crawley knows anything about. I just talked to him in Mantilla, where he's holed up in a big fancy resort hotel while the local maritime people are trying to track down his niece's yacht. He'll meet us at Rangatoa, if we like."

"That will be fine," Zarkon nodded. "What about the geosurvey report?"

"Crawley called his office and told 'em to feed it through to us. Should be coming through anytime," Scorchy said, glancing over at the photofax machine which stood at the end of a row of news service tickers. Just then an attention light flashed on and the photofax rollers began whirling. Scorchy went over to peel off the facsimile papers as they came sliding through the slot.

"All through here, chief," said Menlo. "Law enforcement ginks at Mantilla are welcoming us with bonbons and roses. Say we can fly anything inta them islands up to an' includin' an atom bomb if we wanta. What now?"

"Scorchy, give Menlo the name of Crawley's niece and her fiancé's name as well. Menlo, check them out with Justice in Washington and with the police in Mantilla, just for the sake of thoroughness."

His voice broke off and an expression of calm thoughtfulness crossed his usually immobile features. He was studying the fax copy of the geological survey report from Pacific Mining & Minerals.

"Somethin' innerestin', chief?" demanded Scorchy keenly.

"Hard to say," said Zarkon noncommittally.

"Why the weighty expression, then?" Muldoon asked.

"The name of the geologist who conducted the survey," said Zarkon, handing the papers back. Scorchy peered through them puzzledly. Then he stopped short and uttered an exclamation.

"What's up Short Stuff?" cracked Nick Naldini.

"The name o' the gink did the looksee job on the island," mumbled the bantamweight redhead.

Nick ambled over to look at the copies. "So? 'John James Jones.' Outside of the fact that, with his set of initials, he'll never be likely to pick up the wrong luggage at the airport, what about it?"

"That's the name," announced Scorchy portentously, "of the guy Crawley's niece wants to marry. Interesting!"

As things turned out, Braxton T. Crawley changed his mind, and called the *Skyrocket* on the radiophone to say he would meet them at the Luzon National Airport, on the outskirts of Mantilla. It was Prince Zarkon himself who took the call; when he returned the receiver to its cradle, a thoughtful expression made his normally impassive features somber. He reported the change in plans without comment. Scorchy, however, was inquisitive.

"So how come, chief?" demanded the feisty little bantamweight. "How come Mantilla instead of Rangatoa?"

"Mr. Crawley's annoyed," replied the Ultimate Man musingly. "When he attempted to rent a boat for the trip to the island, none of the locals would ferry him for any price. They seem to feel there is a jinx on the place. I gather that word of the volcano monster has begun to spread."

Ace Harrigan, taking a brief respite from the controls

while the automatic pilot flew the aircraft, cocked one eyebrow quizzically.

"Oh yeah?" He whistled. "I thought this Braxton was a pretty big gun out in the islands. Pacific Mining and Minerals is the largest corporation working in the Luzon group, according to our walking encyclopedia over there," he said, obviously referring to Doc Jenkins. "If the local Rockefeller can't swing a boat rental, things must be getting mighty tense out there!"

"Hrmph," sniffed Menlo Parker suspiciously. "Why can't he use one of his own company's boats, chief? Doesn't sound quite kosher to me . . ."

Zarkon shook his head. "Come now, Menlo, be reasonable. Pacific Mining and Minerals doesn't keep a resident fleet out there in the islands, you know. The ore boats themselves are huge cargo craft; to divert one to use as a private ferry would cost the company thousands of dollars. It's quite likely that the firm owns a few light skiffs and motorboats, but those channels are tricky, I understand; and Rangatoa is probably beyond their safety range. It doesn't matter: we can as easily land at Mantilla, to pick up Crawley, as at Rangatoa."

So they did just that. It was dawn when the *Skyrocket* came down in Mantilla Bay and taxied in toward shore. Zarkon had called ahead to apprise Crawley to come out in a skiff, as they would be landing on the retractable seaplane landing gear rather than on the airport landing strip, in order to save time. The Omega men peered out at palm-fringed shoreline and the glistening white towers of luxury resort hotels which lined the bay. Soon a small motorboat put out to meet them. Its ensign, fluttering in the breeze, marked it as property of Pacific Mining & Minerals. The little craft carved a white half-circle against the rich blue-green of the bay as it slowed to approach the open door in the flanks of the rocketplane. In a few moments Crawley and his luggage were lifted aboard —both of them requiring considerable assistance in this, as it happened.

Scorchy's eyes popped and his lips framed a silent whistle. "Good thing we didn't take aboard any ballast," he wisecracked to Nick Naldini. "If we had, we'd'a hadta dump it over th' side!"

Braxton T. Crawley turned out to be the fattest man any of them had ever seen, this side of a circus sideshow. He was, almost literally, as wide as he was tall. In fact, as skinny Menlo Parker later remarked, he was *wider*, since he was so lacking in height as to hardly come up to Menlo's own armpit.

"At last," drawled Nick Naldini sardonically, "we meet somebody smaller than Pint-Size, here. Cheer up, Muldoon! Eat your spinach and there's hope for you yet!"

Braxton T. Crawley heard none of this comic byplay, for he was puffing and blowing like a beached walrus while the men in the boat heaved and shoved and pushed to get him into the airplane. Once in, he wrung Zarkon's hand limply, then collapsed in a seat while mopping his round red face vigorously with a bandanna handkerchief only a shade or two darker than his own scarlet visage.

"Guy's got a head like a tomato," grinned Ace Harrigan to Doc Jenkins. "Got about as much hair on it, too."

"Hush up, he'll hear you," chuckled Doc in a whisper. But, if a bit impolite, Ace Harrigan's remark was not far from the truth. For the wealthy industrialist was as bald as an egg, and his bright china-blue eyes lacked eyebrows and even eyelashes, and his cheeks were clean-shaven. When he removed the bandanna from his perspiring face, however, something unexpected in the way of hirsute adornment came into view. It was a walrus mustache so huge and whiskery you would hardly have believed that even a bandanna could have concealed it.

"Wow!" breathed Scorchy Muldoon in awe. "Wax that set of lip-ornaments up and you could rent yerself to a bicycle as a set o' spare handlebars!"

Nick Naldini, whose own carefully waxed and pointed mustachios and trim little Mephisto-type Imperial were a point of personal pride, and often earned him a crack from Scorchy Muldoon, was too impressed to respond.

"Holy Houdini," the ex-magician gasped feebly. "It's like all the hair on his head had migrated to his upper lip!"

"Yeah, sure is," swore Muldoon feelingly. "If the mining business ever gives out, fatso over there can lease out his upper lip for a soup-strainer."

"Please strap yourself in, Mr. Crawley," said Zarkon as he and Doc Jenkins closed and sealed the cabin door. "My pilot will be taking off immediately."

"Can't take off any too soon t' please *me*, Prince!" boomed Braxton T. Crawley in a surprising foghorn voice. "Guess you fellers ain't heard the latest? Thet dang-fool niece o' mine! Cuss her cantankerous ways! Thet fortune-huntin' college boy she went and got herself engaged to—against her uncle's own wishes, too!—seems he's right smack in the middle of all thet trouble out on Rangatoa—got himself *vanished* somehow, too!"

"What's that?" demanded Zarkon sharply. "I gather that you refer to your former survey geologist, John James Jones—"

"Thet's the guy," roared the fat man in his bass-fiddle voice. "Dang-fool name, *I* always said!—"

"You say the young man has vanished?" continued Zarkon. The red-faced man nodded vigorously, full cheeks flapping like a pair of scarlet and well-inflated bladders.

"Into thin air!" he boomed heartily. "Not that I mind if the young idiot wants to git himself into a peck o' trouble —once he's off the payroll, let'm do anything he dang-fool *wants,* I always say!—But Fooey, wellsir, thet's another kettle o' fish—"

"'Fooey?'" repeated Zarkon questioningly.

"My niece—short for 'Phoenicia'—her baby name for herself—also her favorite cussword, if you can call *thet* a cussword," rumbled the little fat man in his scowling, belligerent way, walrus mustache bristling.

"I don't understand," murmured Prince Zarkon. "You say your niece went to Rangatoa to meet her fiancé—?"

"Right!" roared Crawley, blue eyes ablaze with indignation. "Serves her right; thet fortune-huntin' young pup she *thinks* she's in love with got carried off by thet dang-fool murdering monster, or whatever it is—but thet's not the worst of it: *now my niece has up and disappeared, too!*"

CHAPTER 6

A Scream in the Night

After picking up their new passenger, Braxton T. Crawley, the Omega men set out on the last leg of their trip to the island of Rangatoa. Once the fat, red-faced man with the enormous walrus mustache was safely aboard and his luggage was stowed away, Ace Harrigan swung the big rocketplane around and taxied out of Mantilla Bay. The silvery nose of the *Skyrocket* pointed into the depthless blue of a Pacific morning, and the experimental aircraft rose into the sky, folding its pontoons.

Having delivered himself of the news that both John James Jones and his headstrong niece, Fooey Mulligan, had now mysteriously vanished, the fat millionaire sat by the cabin window, peering moodily down on the islands of the Luzon Group as they swept by beneath the rocketplane.

"Lot's o' history down there," the red-faced man rumbled through his walrus mustache to Menlo Parker, who had taken the seat next to him. Neither happened to think about what an amusing picture they provided, contrasted with each another: Braxton T. Crawley, who was nearly about as wide as he was tall, and frail little Menlo Parker, with his spindly arms, bony chest, and skinny shanks.

Indeed, the oddly mismatched duo resembled two of

the standard human oddities often found in circus sideshows—the World's Fattest Man and the Human Skeleton.

"Hmph? History?" grumbled Menlo, who was thinking about something mathematical and was barely listening to his neighbor.

"Shore!" boomed Crawley heartily, cocking one pudgy thumb at the island passing directly astern at that moment. "Thet there is Shark Head Island, for instance. Ever hear tell of it?"

"Can't say that I have," murmured Menlo indifferently.

"Oh yeah? Famous pirate stronghold, once upon a time," said Braxton T. Crawley, with much the same proprietary air as that of a resident pointing out sights of local interest to a visitor "Notorious Chinese pirate, name of Tom Too, used to have his main hangout down thar. A real hellion, thet boy! Like to nearabouts take over all these here islands, he did! Came to a real sticky end, though . . ."

Menlo was working energy-transference equations in his head—his favorite form of mental relaxation, when bored—so he merely nodded without listening. Braxton T. Crawley seemed to take it for granted that Menlo's silence was due to his rapt fascination with Crawley's words. He continued pointing out and discussing the local points of interest, making verbal commentary on each, while Menlo, no longer even pretending to listen, politely nodded from time to time.

Ace brought the big rocketplane down in the waters offshore Rangatoa and the Omega men and Braxton T. Crawley went ashore by means of inflatable rubber rafts. Señor Valdez met them on the beach, at the head of a native delegation of the island's leading citizens.

The courtly hidalgo was sufficiently impressed just at meeting the celebrated Prince Zarkon and his famous team of adventurers; when he realized the identity of the seventh member of their party, none other than Braxton T. Crawley, head of Pacific Mining & Minerals, he was flabbergasted. But the blood of ancient Spanish Dons flowed in his aristocratic veins. Mastering his emotions, Señor Valdez greeted them with the exquisite manners and gracious hospitality of his race.

Never before in its history, Señor Valdez assured them as he ushered them to seats on the veranda of the trading post, had the unimportant little island of Rangatoa played host to such distinguished celebrities. The day of their arrival would be long remembered.

Zarkon politely sipped the tea poured for them by Señor Valdez' housekeeper. The amenities out of the way, the Man from Tomorrow got directly to the point, inquiring into the disappearance of Braxton T. Crawley's niece, and her fiancé.

The Spaniard shrugged helplessly.

"But it is most regrettable, señor; alas, the señorita has not yet been found," he said in his native tongue, which language Zarkon spoke and understood as easily as he did English. "The first we knew that aught was amiss was the screams in the night—"

"Screams?"

"But yes, señor! From the mountain, or so it seemed to us. We could see nothing, it being night and the moon shining in such-and-such a manner that the side of the mountain which faces our village was completely hidden in darkness. But there were shots, first, as I recollect—"

"What kind of shots?" inquired Zarkon.

Again Señor Valdez shrugged. "I, who know but little of such matters, cannot say. But not the shots of a rifle;

no; had such been the firearm employed, the explosions would surely have been louder and more resonant. The sounds were that of the firing, I believe, of a small weapon, a little gun, a—what is the word?—oh, yes: a *peestol.* The kind of weapon which a well-bred young señorita might well have carried."

"Dang-fool niece of mine packed a little teeny-weeny pearl-handled revolver in her handbag," rumbled Braxton T. Crawley in his grumpy, bullfrog voice.

"That is it, Señor Crawley." Valdez nodded quickly. "That is the sort of gun it sounded like to me!"

"And then you heard screams, coming from up on the mountain?" repeated Zarkon.

Valdez nodded vigorously. "But yes! Immediately upon the heels of the gunshots—"

"How many shots were there—did you count them?"

"Alas, such were the echoes that bounced down the slopes of the volcano, and so rapidly did the *peestol* fire, that it is hard to say. Perhaps five, perhaps six, perhaps even more."

"In other words, the gal emptied her revolver at something an' when it didn't stop comin' and she ran outta ammunition, she cut loose with some good, old-fashioned hollerin'," Scorchy Muldoon commented sotto voce to Nick Naldini, who sat beside him on the rattan veranda chairs.

"And what happened after this?" inquired Zarkon.

"The screaming, it stopped. All at once, as if cut off by some force," murmured Señor Valdez. "Me, I jumped out of my hammock and rushed to the room of the young señorita, so as to ascertain if she was safe. You will understand, gentlemen, that I did not know at once that it was the young señorita who had fired the gunshots and who had screamed. It could have been a woman of the village."

"But it was Miss Mulligan who had fired the pistol and done the screaming, wasn't it?" Zarkon pressed. "At least, you think so, because she was not in her room and was nowhere to be found?"

"That is precisely the case," agreed Valdez. "The door to the señorita's room was still locked, but the window was open. I assume, señors, that the young lady was carried off by that exit."

Zarkon got to his feet.

"Show us the room."

Señor Valdez led them to the small guest-room which had formerly been occupied by Miss Fooey Mulligan. Zarkon swiftly searched the room, his keen black eyes missing no slightest detail. He found nothing of interest, or seemed not to, at any rate, from his impassive demeanor. Then he turned to the window, examining the sill through a powerful lens he generally carried with him. Opening the window, he peered out, searching the ground with quick eyes. Then he lithely climbed out, jumped down to the ground, and looked about. The others followed, although Señor Valdez, who was too old, or too dignified, or both, to climb out of windows, and the girl's uncle, who was much too fat, made their exit by means of the door, going down the veranda steps to join Zarkon and his aides underneath the girl's window.

"What do you think, chief?" inquired Ace Harrigan quietly, when Zarkon had finished studying the ground beneath the window. The crack test-pilot knew his boss had eyes trained to observe the slightest clue, like a latter-day Sherlock Holmes, and could track his quarry through forest, meadow, or jungle with the eaglelike facility of the Last of the Mohicans.

"Miss Mulligan was not carried off, but left the trading post under her own steam," said Zarkon firmly. "Before doing so, she changed her clothes, donning whipcord breeches and riding-boots—"

"How on earth can you know *that*?" demanded Braxton T. Crawley in astonishment.

"Because the lilac-colored frock she wore when she arrived is neatly laid out on the bed, and the rest of her clothes are still unpacked, except for the contents of the small zipper bag beside the nightstand," said Zarkon. "The fact that she put on boots is evident from the bootjack she removed from the case, used, and put down on the floor beside the high-heeled shoes she had been wearing. A young woman of fashion generally wears riding-breeches with boots of that kind, and they are invariably of whipcord. A small scrap of whipcord material is caught in the corner of the windowsill, torn from her breeches when she skinned over the sill. And the heel prints in the soft earth under the window, where she landed after jumping down, are the sort of heels wherewith ladies' riding boots are fitted."

"Wow," said the fat man, highly impressed.

Zarkon pointed across the fields in the direction of the slope of the mountain.

"From the footprints I have thus far found, she went in that direction, and rather quickly. Also, from the absence of any other prints, it would seem that she was alone."

"In other words, señor, she was not abducted by the monster? asked Señor Valdez bewilderedly. "The señorita went of her own free accord?"

"So it would seem," said Zarkon. "What lies in that direction?"

"Nothing, señor . . . that is to say, well, the *mountain* itself, of course . . . but nothing else."

"And if you continue in that direction?"

"The other side of the mountain—"

"And on the other side?"

"Why, nothing . . . the further slope, then the edge of the swamp—ah! of course, I see it now—what a fool I am not to have thought of it before!—on the other slope, down at the foot of the mountain, built at the very edge of the swamp, is the little hut in which the Yankee, her betrothed, lived—that is where she must have been going!"

Zarkon nodded: he gathered that the girl, anxious and concerned about John James Jones, had pluckily determined to investigate the matter for herself, and had taken the most obvious shortcut to his camp. That is, while climbing the mountain and going down the other side was somewhat more difficult than going the long way around, at least she didn't have to wade through the jungle in order to get there, which would save her time; and, if all she had with her was a small, pearl-handled revolver, it was easy to understand why Phoenicia Mulligan would prefer climbing a mountain, even a volcano, to struggling through a jungle at night.

Zarkon turned to his men and swiftly began giving instructions.

"Ace, Doc, take the rubber boats back to the *Skyrocket* and unload the equipment cases; I imagine Señor Valdez will let us use his store room to keep them in—"

"But yes, it will be a pleasure!" cried the old gentleman.

"Menlo, you stay here to supervise the unpacking. Nick and Scorchy, you two circle around the base of the mountain and see if you can find this shack or hut where John James Jones was staying before he disappeared. When you get there, stay there, unless I call for help," he said, tapping the small beltpack he wore, which contained a miniaturized radio set.

"Right you are, chief; a little action at last!" chortled the Pride of the Muldoons, rubbing his hands together briskly.

"Very well," nodded Nick Naldini. "But what are you going to do, chief?"

Zarkon inclined his head in the direction of the mountain's smoking crest.

"I will be tracking Miss Mulligan," he said. And without another word the Ultimate Man went across the fields, approached the base of the volcano, and began to ascend it at a pace so swift and easy you would have sworn that the almost sheer, cliff-like face was as flat as a ballroom floor.

Señor Valdez and Braxton T. Crawley, who were standing side by side, stared after the Nemesis of Evil. Both the gentlemanly, silver-haired old hidalgo and the fat, red-faced industrialist with the enormous walrus mustache wore almost identical expressions which denoted slack-jawed, open-mouthed awe.

"Amazin' young feller," gasped Braxton T. Crawley in a feeble voice, after a time.

"*Madre de Dios,*" swore Señor Valdez feelingly, "he is certainly that."

Nick Naldini grinned his wicked, satanic grin. He exchanged a wink with Scorchy.

"You gentleman," he announced in his suave, whiskey-rough voice, "don't know the half of it!"

Nor did they, of course.

CHAPTER 7

The Stone Monster

Jungles were not precisely the sort of terrain Scorchy Muldoon would have picked to stroll about in. His natural habitat was the streets of the city. There, one seldom if ever had to contend with tangled roots, drooping vines, thorny bushes, or sodden swampy ground. Hence the red-headed little boxer found the going tough.

Thorn-edged leaves slashed at his legs. The loop of a dangling vine settled like a noose around his neck. No sooner had he pulled loose from the offensively affectionate liana than he stepped ankle-deep in a puddle of squelching ooze. These difficulties triggered a stream of invective from the little prize-fighter to which Nick Naldini listened with rapt admiration. When Scorchy "got his Irish up"—as he would have put it—and lost his temper, his command of verbal vituperation would have put to shame the most sulphur-tongued of longshoremen.

"What's the matter, boy?" quipped the lanky vaudevillian with a nasty grin, as Scorchy came cussing and dripping out of the swampy puddle. "I'd've thought all this greenery would remind you of the Auld Sod. Especially the boggy places."

Scorchy fumed, wiping the mud off his shoes. "Ireland has its bogs, I'm not denyin'," he grumbled. "But nothin' loike this! Why d'you suppose th' chief wanted us t' come the long way 'round, anyway?"

"Probably in order to circumvent the problem of omni-ovaciousness," replied Nick with another of those sarcastic grins of his.

Scorchy blinked. "How's that?" he inquired. The lanky magician had, on occasion, when prestidigitators were a drug on the market but classical actors were at a premium, trod the boards in a variety of Shakespearian roles. From this, quite possibly, the vaudevillian had developed a taste for jawbreakers such as "omni-ovaciousness," and an outsized vocabulary to match.

"One does not wish to put all one's eggs in the same basket," explained Nick succinctly.

"You mean the chief wants us around in case he has to call up the reserves, but doesn't want us doggin' his footsteps?" said Scorchy, finally getting it.

"That's my guess, Small Change," shrugged the stage magician.

"Then why didn't ya say it loike that in th' first place?" demanded Scorchy, struggling out of another boggy place.

"I keep forgetting I have to cut everything down to words of one syllable when conversing with the culturally deprived," snickered the lanky escape artist.

"Oh yeah?" growled Scorchy belligerently, shoving out his jaw and balling his fists warningly. "Any more o' yer lip, you road-company stand-in fer John Carradine, and I'll be after deprivin' *you* o' sumphin—yer front teeth, t' start with!"

That crack about the distinguished stage and screen artist, John Carradine, stung Nick to the quick; his uncanny resemblance to the star actor was a matter of personal pride. Naldini's long, sallow, lantern-jawed face flushed darkly. He scowled dangerously.

"Why, you pint-size Irish potato, how'd'ja like t' get mashed?" he hissed venomously.

Before long the insults were flying back and forth so hot and heavy that neither Nick nor Scorchy bothered to watch where they were going. And both ended up hip-deep in the bogs.

The cabin which had been home to Phoenicia Mulligan's fiancé, John James Jones, before he disappeared so mysteriously, was nearby. A small deck ran around three sides of it, and it was built partly out over the bog, on pilings. Nick reached up with his long arms, grabbed the deck-rail, and hauled himself, dripping, out of the swampy muck. Scorchy scrambled out soon after, and the two, their quarrel set aside for the moment, rested side by side without conversation, catching their breath and trying to get rid of some of the gooey mud they had walked into.

Nick peered inside the cabin, spotting a folding army cot, a steamer trunk, a collapsible washstand, and a hotplate on a small wall-shelf which also held cans of soup, beef stew, and condensed milk.

The cabin itself was one of those prefabricated huts the US Army had devised for swampy jungle country. Glancing around, Nick gave a disapproving sniff: such accommodations were a bit too Spartan in their simplicity and too primitive, as far as the creature comforts went, to satisfy him.

"Anything?" inquired Scorchy, peering around him at the almost-empty room. The lanky magician shrugged.

"You take a look around outside, you know, footprints or whatever, while I search in here," he suggested.

Scorchy rather surprisingly agreed without argument. The two men were so used to automatically *dis*agreeing with each other, on every conceivable point that might arise, that such a giving-in on Scorchy's part was just a bit unusual. The fact of the matter was that the little Irishman had glimpsed something up on the slope of the mountain that looked promising, and he wanted to be the first to discover it, whatever it was. If he could find an important clue to the disappearance of the young geologist all by himself, that would mean he would be one up on the vaudevillian. Making coups at Nick's expense was food and drink to Scorchy Muldoon.

While the magician poked around inside the cabin, the little Irishman clambered up the side of the mountain a ways. What he had seen from the foot of the volcano had looked promising and might be important—a patch of scruffy grass, burnt black as soot. When he reached it, he found the soil disturbed nearby, the marks of a clawing hand, and—

Scorchy's lips framed a silent whistle. A footprint, by golly! Or—*was* it? For the mark looked too huge and flat to be that . . . more like the print of some enormous creature whose paw-pads were larger than those of a bear. He bent to examine the marks more closely.

So absorbed was Scorchy in his detective-work that he did not see the strange, lumbering monstrosity descending the mountain with slow and awkward steps. But the huge, massive creature saw him.

And crept up behind the unsuspecting little boxer, who did not realize anything was there until he smelled the odor of hot stone, and turned, to see *horror*.

So swiftly had Prince Zarkon sent his men on their several errands, and departed from the scene himself, to climb the volcanic mountain in search of the missing heiress, that Señor Valdez had no opportunity to offer his services in any capacity.

It occurred to the courtly Spaniard, a bit later, while the village boys were helping the Omega men to fetch ashore their cases of equipment, which were to be stored in the back room of the trading-post, that neither Naldini nor Muldoon had much of an idea where the hut of the young Yankee geologist was located. Without some careful direction, the two Americans might easily go astray and end up in the swamp, he thought to himself, a trifle guiltily, wishing that he had volunteered to guide them around the base of the mountain.

Well, there was no time like the present for repairing such omissions, thought the old gentleman. Leaving his husky villagers to see the equipment cases safely stored away, Señor Valdez crossed the planted fields and entered the edge of the jungle. The marks of Scorchy's blundering feet were plainly obvious, so the Spaniard knew exactly how the two Omega men had traveled.

He made it through the tangled jungle far more swiftly and easily than had Scorchy Muldoon and Nick Naldini. For one thing, this was very far from being the first time that Señor Valdez had traveled on foot through the jungles; and for another, of course, he knew exactly where he was going and where all the shortcuts were. Consequently, he circled the base of the mountain and emerged at the edge of the swamp where John James Jones had built his hut not long after Nick and Scorchy reached it. Or almost, at any rate.

For Señor Valdez had nearly gotten out of the jungle when he heard an unearthly screeching, followed by the hiss and chatter of some manner of gunfire with which he was unfamiliar. Señor Valdez did not know that Prince

Zarkon's lieutenants were armed with special firearms of the Prince's own design, weapons which fired mercy-bullets of hard rubber by means of compressed air. That explained the peculiar gunshots he heard.

The screeching itself had come from Scorchy Muldoon.

"*Madre de Dios!*" gasped the old hidalgo, paling at the sounds of squalling and gunfire. He redoubled his efforts and emerged from the edge of the jungle just about the same time that Nick Naldini, white to the lips, came leaping out of the hut to see what had happened to his pal.

"Scorchy! *Scorchy!*" yelped Nick, waving his own pistol about frantically. His hoarse voice was raw with urgency, and there was so much alarm audible in his tones that Señor Valdez blinked in puzzlement. Since the first moment they had landed on the shores of Rangatoa, the pint-sized little Irishman and the lanky Italian had been virtually at each other's throats. Señor Valdez could have sworn that the two Omega men were the deadliest of enemies: now Nick Nadkini seemed so upset at the thought of Scorchy being hurt or attacked, you would have thought them the dearest of friends. The old hidalgo shrugged in bafflement; very often the ways of Yankees were beyond his comprehension.

Muldoon came into view, looking a bit shaken but otherwise unhurt.

"What happened?" demanded Nick, scrambling up the mountain.

"Cheez, I dunno," mumbled Muldoon a bit vaguely. "I wuz just examinin' this-here ledge fer clues, when—"

He waved his pistol in the general direction of the spot he had glimpsed earlier from below. Nick blinked thoughtfully at the burnt spot, the torn earth, and the huge Abominable Snowman-size pad-print. Señor Valdez followed Scorchy's gesture. Suddenly his furrowed brow cleared.

"Is it that you mistook these marks for a clue into the evanishment of Señor Jones?" he inquired eagerly.

"Why, sure," mumbled Scorchy in surprise. "What else c'd they be?"

"But no," declared the silver-haired old gentleman in a most positive tone of voice. "These marks were made by the unfortunate youth I dispatched hither yesterday, to apprise Señor Jones of the arrival of his fiancée, Señorita Mulligan."

"Hey, you mean the kid that wuz th' monster's *second* victim?" cried Scorchy, his voice eloquent with disappointment. "Daggone it, here I thought I hadda clue!"

"Alas, it was here that the body of Jimmie Okawa was found," admitted Señor Valdez. Scorchy looked crestfallen.

"Never mind that now, What was all the yellin' and shootin' about?" snarled Nick Naldini. He was furious that Scorchy might have heard him calling out his name with such alarm and anguish in his voice as to suggest a fondness for the little runt. If Scorchy had noticed same, Nick knew gloomily he would be twitted unmercifully about it later.

Fortunately for Nick, Scorchy had other things on his mind.

"Well, I saw the hoodoo's been doin' all these-here murders," admitted the little fighter in a small voice.

"You *did?*" cried Nick, pop-eyed with amazement. "Where? What was he doing? What did he look like?"

"Yes, and, more to the point," interjected Señor Valdez keenly, "where did he go?"

Scorchy waved vaguely off to one side.

"Dunno about that, but he wuz comin' down the side o' th' volcano, begorra," he mumbled shame-facedly. "Scared th' living daylights outa me, too. I ripped off a few shots, but nuttin' happened—dang these here mercy-bullets, anyway! 'F'ya don't get 'em in th' right spot, they don't do no gosh-darned good at all!" He gulped, and added feebly, "Not that you could do much t' th' critter I seen, even with real bullets . . ."

"What does *that* mean?" growled Nick exasperatedly.

Scorchy windmilled his arms.

"He wuz big as a house, he wuz, an' wide as a barn! Din't have any face on 'im, or any neck at all! I couldn't see much because he was so hot he was steamin' . . . but I saw enough t' know one thing fer sure," he added grimly.

"What's that?"

"He's all made outa stone," said Scorchy in a thin voice. "Like a living idol o' th' heathen. A thing of red-hot stone, what walks like a man!"

Nick licked his thin lips with a pointed tongue, tightened his grip on the pistol, and darted an apprehensive glance about the side of the mountain, as if half-expecting to see the lumbering stone monster come to life at any moment.

A chill breeze was blowing up his spine.

Despite their continual feuding, the lanky magician knew Scorchy through and through, from his peppery temper to the staunch, manly soul in him. Scorchy was not given to panic; neither did he prevaricate.

If he said he saw a walking stone monster, then that was what he saw.

There was a moment of speechless silence there on the slope of the monster-haunted island. Scorchy and Nick exchanged a long glance, then looked at Señor Valdez.

The silver-haired old Spaniard crossed himself and seemed to be praying.

CHAPTER 8

Now You See It—

While Prince Zarkon's rapid and apparently effortless ascent of the steep slope of the mountain had seemed miraculous to Mr. Braxton T. Crawley, the only miraculous thing about it from Zarkon's own point of view was that this was the route taken by the young woman, seemingly by her own choice.

For the first thirty feet or so the rockface rose almost as smooth and sheer as a cliff. Then it broke into a series of ledges that were considerably easier to climb. Zarkon, who had learned the art of mountain-climbing from skilled and veteran Sherpa guides in Tibet, found the ascent easy enough. But it said something for Miss Phoenicia Mulligan's character that she had chosen this difficult place for her ascent of Mount Rangatoa.

Obviously, the young lady liked danger, enjoyed meeting a challenge, and was "just too dang-fool stubborn" (as her Uncle would probably have phrased it) to turn aside in favor of an easier route.

There was no doubt in Zarkon's mind that Fooey Mulligan had in fact come by this way. The signs of her ascent were clearly visible for those with eyes keen enough to notice them and to understand what they implied. Here a pebble, long in place, had recently been dislodged by fumbling, groping hands, for the raw stone beneath where it had lain so long was not as worn and discolored as the stone around the place. And over here a smear of fresh boot-polish showed plainly against the rock where the girl had scraped her boot in struggling for a foot-hold.

Indeed, pinched in a crack of stone, Zarkon even found a long, silky strand of bright gold hair. It was still supple and fragrant with the odor of a popular shampoo used by young women of fashion.

Zarkon climbed the side of the volcano until he was near the top. He could tell that he was getting close to the crater from the increasing warmth of the stone under his hands and the growing stench of sulphur on the air. The warmth of the stone was not a surface warmth from sunlight, but came from beneath: volcanic heat, obviously. Doc Jenkins had told them that Mount Rangatoa was an active volcano, although it had not had a major eruption for generations. But you could have known that without prior information, for a plume of white smoke drifted from the crest, tossed and torn on the fresh morning breeze.

As he climbed, Zarkon's eyes were busy. They roamed hither and thither, noting every sign of the girl's passage. They missed nothing, those sharp black eyes.

Near the crest the slope flattened out. He no longer had to crouch to climb, but could stand erect and walk the gentle slope that led up to the mouth of the volcano. It was of no great height, Mount Rangatoa; you could climb it easily in ten or fifteen minutes, even without the veteran experience that was Zarkon's.

Obviously, from the way the slope sudenly flattened out near the top, the peak of the volcano had fallen in, collapsing into the crater many times during the past.

This had caused a broad and fairly level zone around the mouth of the volcano, greatly reducing its height.

Zarkon walked farther up the mountain, studying the ground. No grass grew here, or, rather, such few patches of scruffy turf as did were withered by the heat. The stone was hot under foot and the patches of grass were crisped.

Here Phoenicia Mulligan had stopped suddenly. Zarkon's eyes narrowed thoughtfully as he read her actions in the scuff of a boot, a pebble dislodged from its niche—marks which would hardly have been noticeable to anything other than his own carefully-trained eyes.

Here she had started to run.

Here she had been—attacked?

A brassy glint caught his eye. He bent and picked up a fresh cartridge from beneath a rocky shelf. He held it to his nostrils. It had been ejected quite recently.

Searching the ground for further clues, he strolled nearly to the top.

Then he stopped quite suddenly and froze, motionless.

For a voice spoke from behind him.

"Put your hands up or I'll put a slug through you," the voice said. It sounded quite hard and determined, that voice. Zarkon slowly elevated his hands.

"Now turn around so I can see you. Slowly!" the voice gave further directions. Zarkon did as he was told.

A gasp sounded. A voice, clearly feminine, said, faintly, "You? But what are *you* doing here?"

Zarkon relaxed imperceptibly. He even allowed a slight smile to play around the corners of his mouth.

"Looking for you, I imagine," he said lightly. "Miss Phoenicia Mulligan, I presume?"

A figure came into view from behind a large rock. It was that of a devastatingly attractive young woman in riding-boots and breeches and a khaki safari shirt that did nothing to conceal the curves of a lithe and supple girlish figure. They were all in exactly the right places, those curves. Even Zarkon, no ladies' man by any stretch of the imagination, could not help noticing the fact.

The girl peered at him blankly. Her thick length of bright blond hair was tangled and windblown. There was a raw scrape on one cheek and a smudge of dirt on her small, tip-tilted smidgen of a nose. Her eyes were large and lakewater-blue, framed in thick black lashes that owed nothing, or very little, to the use of mascara.

"How do *you* know *me*?" demanded the girl, waving the small, pearl-handled revolver. Noticing it, she tucked it away in its holster at her belt, absently.

Zarkon shrugged. "I am more interested in the reverse of that question," he admitted.

She blinked puzzledly at him; then her expression cleared, and he voiced a little laugh.

"Oh, I see what you mean! How did I recognize you as Prince Zarkon of Novenia, the head of the Omega organization?"

"Precisely," Zarkon nodded.

She shrugged airily. "Oh, fooey! That's no big secret. A young man I sometimes date works for the FBI in their Knickerbocker City office. The last time I had dinner with him, he was simply raving about some case of yours. Seems you had just single-handedly broken up a sinister Chinese tong or something. Nobody in the law enforcement business had any idea or even realized that one of those old-fashioned secret societies from the Twenties was still around; but you found the headquarters and went in alone to beard the arch-villain in his lair, or words to that effect!"

Zarkon said nothing, his face expressionless. But he felt

distinctly uncomfortable: he didn't enjoy being praised for his work. Of course, he remembered the case to which the young lady was referring, but he didn't care to make any comment.*

The girl laughed a bit breathlessly. "My boy-friend was impressed by this feat of yours; he raved about you all through dinner. He simply couldn't talk of anything else. At first, quite naturally, I was rather piqued. After all, a girl expects to be paid attention to! Eventually, he got my curiosity aroused. I bugged him until he agreed to show me a picture of you. I wanted to see what such a superman looked like!"

Zarkon (who had a marked aversion to the camera, and studiously avoided being photographed on every possible occasion, on the theory that a man in a profession as dangerous as his works much more safely when his enemies don't know what he looks like) frowned.

"A picture?" he repeated disapprovingly. The girl nodded, blond curls tumbling about slim, rounded shoulders.

"Sure!" She grinned. "Seems the FBI keeps a pretty complete dossier on you. My friend sneaked it out one evening and let me look at it. That's how I recognized you when you turned around just now. Oh . . . sorry about the gun, by the way. It was empty, anyway."

"Because you fired it at the volcano monster?" he asked.

She looked surprised.

"How did you know that? Come to think of it, what are you *doing* here, anyway? And how did you know who I was?"

"I climbed the mountain hoping to find you," he ex-

* The case to which Phoenicia Mulligan refers is one of those I have novelized through the active cooperation of Omega. See the book *Invisible Death,* recently published by Doubleday.—LC

plained patiently. "I knew you were here because Señor Valdez told me you had vanished during the night, and I followed your tracks here. I didn't have a description of you, but I hardly assumed there would likely be two young white women climbing about the mountain at the same time."

She absorbed this thoughtfully.

"Golly, I'm sure sorry to have worried Señor Valdez! He's such a nice old gentleman; very hospitable. Now that you're here, too, p'raps you will help me find my fiancé, John—"

"—James Jones," he finished for her, with another rare smile. There was something about Miss Phoenicia Mulligan that made Zarkon want to smile, although generally he was very sober and serious and maintained an impassive expression around women. She was so plucky and resourceful, so natural and outspoken: a touch of the tomboy, but with more than a bit of spice and sauce mixed in.

In a word, girls such as Fooey Mulligan were rather a new experience for Prince Zarkon. He didn't quite know how to act in her company. And this, too, was a new experience. He wasn't at all sure he liked feeling so ever-so-slightly confused and off balance and flustered.

"How'd you know *that?*" the girl demanded interestedly.

"Your fiancé's name, and the fact that he's been missing since yesterday? From your Uncle, Braxton T. Crawley."

A mutinous glint flashed in Fooey's big blue eyes.

"Uncle Braxton is *here?*" she asked hotly.

"He met us in Mantilla, and we flew him out to the island," Zarkon admitted.

The girl bristled, then wilted. "Oh, fooey! He *would* come butting in, just when things start happening! Guess

I'd better go down and face the music," she said glumly. "I'm ready if you are, Prince."

Zarkon nodded and took her arm to help her down the steep part of the slope. But just then there came to his ears two sounds he easily recognized. One was the inimitable squall of Scorchy Muldoon in a fight. The other was the sibilant firing of one of the mercy-guns he made his lieutenants carry.

"What's that?" asked Phoenicia Mulligan, jumping at the unexpected sounds.

"One of my men, in trouble! Stay here," said Zarkon, briefly. He whipped around the rock, ran with light and rapid strides to the lip of the crater, and vanished into the plume of rising vapors. So swiftly did the golden man in gunmetal gray move, once he was in motion, that he literally flashed out of the girl's sight.

She stared after him, open-mouthed, for a long moment.

Then her small, firm chin hardened willfully.

"If he thinks he's going to leave *me* behind when the fun gets started," Phoenicia Mulligan said between gritted teeth, "he has another think coming!"

With a determined stride the blond girl climbed to the edge of the crater, circled it, and started down the opposite slope.

Monster or no monster!

Zarkon in time would learn that such as Fooey Mulligan simply would not be left behind when the mystery thickened and things started happening right and left.

It took more than a murdering ogre of walking red-hot stone to keep the likes of Phoenicia Mulligan out of trouble!

The young lady had a nose for it. She was attracted to

danger in the same manner a honeybear is attracted to honey. You could say that the angelic-looking young lady generally tended to rush in foolishly, where even real angels feared to tread.

But you didn't say so where Fooey Mulligan could hear you.

CHAPTER 9

—And Now You Don't!

Scorchy was boiling mad. His blue eyes were fairly spitting sparks.

"Faith, an' Oi been a-tellin' ya," he said, sizzling. "The craytur' wuz right there on the trail—right there where y'do be standin', ya long drink a water, yez!"

"Then where did it go?" asked Nick Naldini, not at all unreasonably. "Walking stone ogres just don't vanish into thin— Hey, chief, Scorchy's been hitting the hootch again. This time he's seeing monsters!"

Prince Zarkon had just come into view, rapidly descending the side of the volcano by a winding trail. The identical same trail, in fact, that Scorchy had just been pointing out with the most vehement of gestures.

"You saw the creature, then, Scorchy?" demanded the Lord of the Unknown, climbing down to where they stood, with Señor Valdez, by the place where the second island boy had been murdered.

"Aye, that Oi did," snarled the feisty little Irishman. "And it's nary a nip I've been sippin', chief, I'll be promisin' ya! Sure an' y'know I've been on the wagon these many years!"

Whenever Scorchy got upset or excited, he slipped automatically into a mode of speech which Nick Naldini unkindly called his "stage Irishman's brogue." The lanky vaudevillian generally threw in a crack about him sounding like he was trying out for a role in the *Barry Fitzgerald Story,* or something equivalently Hibernian.

It is perhaps attributable to Nick's own excited state of mind that in the present instance he refrained from his usual comment. Instead, the tall magician waved his long arms about for attention.

"What is it, Nick?"

"Scorchy actually *saw* the critter, chief! Says he's big as a house and made of burning rock."

"Is this true, Scorchy?"

The little red-headed fighter gulped and shuddered.

"Sure as Oi'm standin' here on me own two feet," he said shrilly. "Looked loike a gorilla, it did, it did, only twice as broad . . . smokin' all over, it wuz, and runnin' wid dribbles o' molten rock . . . ever' time the craytur' moved, little pieces o' stone'd break off it, sorter, and go clatterin' down . . . faith, chief, it wuz standin' right there where you do be standin' now!"

Zarkon turned to survey the slope of the mountain where the trail zigzagged up to the smoking peak.

"You mean it came down this trail?" he asked incredulously.

Scorchy nodded vigorously.

"Aye, that it did! Sure 'n' Oi emptied me gun right at the varmint, but dint do it no harm, just cracked off a bit more o' that smokin', red-hot rock."

The blond girl stared at the little Irishman blankly. Then she pursed her cupid's-bow of a mouth and made a rude sound. Scorchy assumed an injured expression.

"And is it that ye'd be doubtin' me word, miss?" he growled. She tossed back her long hair with a loud sniff.

"You bet!" declared Phoenicia. "Prince Zarkon and I

just came down that trail like a couple of jack-rabbits. And I can promise you, Red, if there'd been any concrete walking statues of King Kong on the trail, we'd of seen 'em!"

Scorchy's scowl became truculent.

"Me name's not 'Red,'" he snapped. "Aloysius Murphy Muldoon, that's me; and me *friends* call me Scorchy."

Zarkon made no comment, ignoring this byplay. What Phoenicia Mulligan had stated was quite correct; it was hard to see where the monster could have gotten to in so short a time, and they certainly would have seen the thing, had it been anywhere on the trail or near it when they had come down.

There was no point in belaboring the obvious, so Zarkon made no mention of this. His keen eyes were busily searching the trail. He stooped and picked up several small bits of rock. They were remarkably light, crisp and colored dark brown, and were distinctly hot to the touch. He held one up so that Scorchy could see it.

"Was this the kind of rock that cracked loose from the monster's body when he moved?" he inquired.

Scorchy indicated that it was. Nick climbed up to examine the bit of rock, curiously. No geologist, he couldn't identify the stuff.

"You know what it is, chief?"

"Yes," acknowledged Zarkon. "The spume or crust that rises to the surface of a lava lake. It hardens quickly when exposed to air."

"*Lava?* Isn't that the name for molten rock?"

"It is," said Zarkon woodenly. "If the ogre was covered with this stuff so that it dripped off or flaked away whenever he walked, he must have waded through the lava up in the crater. There are no streams of lava on the mountain."

"Molten rock, eh?" marveled Nick Naldini with a low whistle. "Pretty hot stuff, isn't it?"

"About one thousand degrees," said Zarkon without inflection. "Fahrenheit," he added soberly.

They searched the trail from the foot of the mountain to the very peak, finding nothing that was of any use. There were no side trails, no clefts or fissures in the mountainside where the ogre might have concealed itself when Zarkon and Fooey Mulligan came down the trail, and not even any boulders or outcroppings large enough for the monster to have crouched behind. It had simply vanished . . . if not into thin air, then somehow it had melted into the solid rock of the mountain itself.

"Too many dang things and people vanishin' around here for the loikes o' me," declared Scorchy.

"Yeah," drawled Nick Naldini, counting on his fingers. "First, John James Jones, the geologist. Then Braxton T. Crawley's niece, Phoenicia Mulligan. Finally, the troll itself, or whatever you prefer to call the thing. Speaking of number two on the list reminds me—the chief actually found the lost girl. Where were you all night, Miss?"

Phoenicia Mulligan, who sat beside Nick and Scorchy on the ledge, kicking her heels while Zarkon searched the hut of her missing boy-friend, shrugged and yawned sleepily.

"Climbing around the top of that blasted mountain," she declared. "Trying to get another look at the monster, or to find out where it hides itself when it's not creeping up behind people and scaring the living daylights out of 'em."

"Or murdering them with one touch of its red-hot paws," added Nick Naldini in sepulchral tones.

The girl shuddered. "Do you have to keep reminding me of that?" she complained.

Scorchy was interested to find someone who had shared his own frightful experience. "You took a coupla pot-shots at the critter, too, didn't you say?" he asked.

Phoenicia nodded wearily. "Emptied my pistol at the huge lumbering thing," she said. "Not that it did any good, any more than your gun did; and instead of using those trick rubber bullets you guys have, mine were real slugs. Should have been able to stop a rhinoceros the way I was shooting—right smack over the heart. If volcano monsters *have* hearts, that is!"

Nick was preening his Mephistophelian mustachios in a thoughtful manner, his dark eyes hooded.

"You think there's anything to this legend of a fire-devil living under the volcano?" he asked. The girl gave him a level look and snorted contemptuously.

"Aw, fooey! You'll be asking me if I believe in vampires and werewolves next," she griped.

Nick chuckled deprecatingly. Scorchy, however, wasn't so sure. Like most Irishmen, he more than half believed in leprechauns, banshees, and the Little People in general. And it wasn't a very far step from that to volcano devils. He said as much, more to trigger another argument with Nick than as an article of personal belief in the supernatural.

Nick, however, was not in the mood to trade insults with his pint-sized pal. Jet-lag was catching up with the long-legged magician: he smothered a yawn behind polite fingers.

"Well . . . dunno that I believe in monsters," he grumbled, "but *something* is walking around here, and it's not only bulletproof but tough enough to go skinny-dippin' in pools of molten lava. Devil or no devil, it's a monster, all right."

"Oh yeah?" growled Scorchy.

"Yeah," said Nick.

Señor Valdez, sitting nearby and puffing on a long cheroot, cleared his throat, his expression philosophical.

"If the gentlemen do not believe in fire trolls," he murmured, "they should perhaps apprise Tommy Kahua and Jimmie Okawa of their non-existence." There was just the slightest flavor of sarcasm in his tones.

Scorchy blinked sleepily. "Whozzat?" he mumbled.

Nick nudged him with a vicious elbow.

"The two island boys the monster killed yesterday, you Hibernian nitwit," he snarled.

Scorchy flushed scarlet, but said nothing.

Zarkon had completed his search of the hut and the terrain immediately around it, and rejoined them shortly after this discussion. The change in time-zones had caught everybody short on sleep, so he suggested that they return to the village, since they could do no more here.

They trooped back single-file through the jungle, and reached the outskirts of Tarapaho just as the island fishermen were dragging their morning's catch ashore. The sight of those fat, silvery fish reminded Nick and Scorchy that they were ravenously hungry. Or reminded Scorchy, at least. For Nick was constantly hungry, and could stow aboard more victuals than the rest of his comrades put together—and still be ready to send out for hamburgers and French fries half an hour later. Nick's digestive system was often referred to as The Bottomless Pit by his partners-in-crime-fighting. Scorchy sometimes suggested that the lanky vaudevillian possessed the proverbial or legendary "hollow leg."

At any rate, the island boys were delighted to arrange a feed for their distinguished guests. Any excuse for a village feast was welcome in Tarapaho. Life here, one gathered, was dull and routine. A barbeque or a banquet made for a happy break in daily doings. In no time, pits were dug in the sand, charcoal was shoveled in, and fresh fish, wrapped in seaweed, were crackling and popping on the glowing coals, shedding an indescribably mouth-watering aroma on the afternoon air.

Squatting tailor-fashion under the palm trees, their necks bewreathed with chains of pink blossoms set in place by giggling native girls, Scorchy crunched down a huge mouthful of crisp fried fish and took a long, refreshing guzzle of cold, fermented coconut-milk. He wiped his mouth with the back of his hand and sat back, replete, patting his midsection.

"This is the life," he said dreamily.

Nick Naldini, squatting beside him, was digging into a succulent native dish, *kaoliang* cooked with rice, using a carved wooden bowl for a plate. He gave his partner a quizzical sideways glance.

"It *would* be the life," he drawled sourly, "if we didn't have that murdering monster prowling around up there on the mountain."

Phoenicia Mulligan, a good-sized meal tucked away, was seated next to Ace Harrigan. The handsome young aviator was feeding her a line of air-war stories from his career as an air ace over Indochina.

"Thirty-seven enemy planes," she murmured, snuggling next to him cozily, sounding very impressed. "My, my!"

Ace, rather bedazzled by the ease of his conquest, did not notice that every time the gorgeous blonde cuddled closer to his side, she sneaked a glance at Prince Zarkon to see if he was at all discomforted by the way she was hanging on Ace Harrigan's every word with eyelash-fluttering fascination. He seemed oblivious to the act she was putting on.

"How *ever* did you get interested in planes in the first place, Ace?" she murmured cooingly.

"Runs in the family." The pilot grinned. "My dad was one of the big names in aviation pioneering, back in the old days. Ever hear of 'Hop' Harrigan? Oh, he was right up there breaking records with famous guys like Barney Baxter, 'Tailspin Tommy' Tomkins, Bill Barnes, 'Smilin' Jack'—"

Ace's list of aviation pioneers and famous fliers broke off suddenly in mid-name.

For a shrill scream of fear ripped through the drowsy afternoon calm.

Down at the end of the double-row of feasters, one of the native women had leaped to her feet, staring with wide eyes into the edge of the jungle. Now she clapped her hands to her cheeks and shrieked again.

The Omega men and Phoenicia Mulligan came to their feet, food and wooden utensils flying. Zarkon whipped around behind the crowd to where Señor Valdez, his fine aristocratic features tense with alarm, bent over the sobbing woman.

"What's wrong with her?" he snapped sharply. "What is it that she saw that frightened her so?"

"Yeah," boomed Braxton T. Crawley belligerently. The fat man came waddling up behind Prince Zarkon and the gentlemanly old Spaniard. "Dame's hysterical! Sounded like she saw some dang-fool *ghost* or somethin'—"

Señor Valdez, murmuring in the local lingo with the frightened woman, came to his feet, searching the edge of the jungle with worried eyes. Then he pointed into the dense foliage dramatically.

"That is exactly it, señor! The poor woman did indeed see a ghost—*behold!*"

He gestured.

All eyes turned to the gloom of the jungle's edge. Suddenly a chorus of frightened gasps broke from the wide-eyed villagers.

From the thick bushes tottered a frail, disheveled figure with haunted face and staring eyes!

The walking scarecrow wore tattered rags. Dark rings circled his glazed and empty eyes.

He staggered toward them, one skinny arm groping, claw-fingered.

Then he collapsed at their feet.

Braxton T. Crawley turned as pale as milk. His eyes bulged huge. He swallowed something big, making his enormous mustache wobble ludicrously. When he spoke, his voice was a strangled squeak instead of a bullfrog gobble.

"Why, th-thet's—!"

Phoenicia Mulligan cleaved through the crowd and sank to her knees beside the ragged figure.

"*John James Jones!*" she cried.

CHAPTER 10

Back from the Grave

It was indeed the young American whose disappearance had touched off a sequence of inexplicable events. Braxton T. Crawley identified the young man in quite positive terms: this was the survey geologist who had worked for his company here in the Luzon islands before his unwelcome attentions to Miss Phoenicia Mulligan—unwelcome to Phoenicia's Uncle, that is; certainly not unwelcome to the young lady herself!—had earned him dismissal as being a scoundrelly young fortune-hunter.

Crawley was not entirely the hot-headed domestic tyrant, however. The fat, red-faced industrialist with the walrus mustache soon displayed that he had a heart of—well, if not exactly of gold, at least the vital organ was composed of one of the softer metals. For he expressed troubled concern over the emaciated condition of the young geologist, and went on record as intending to hire "the best dang-fool sawbones money can buy in these islands" to restore the youth to his former robust condition of health.

They carried the young man into the trading-post and Zarkon fetched his medical kit from the equipment cases in Señor Valdez' storeroom and checked the youth over. It would appear that prolonged exposure, to say nothing of shock and, quite simply, terror, had reduced the young man to a condition resembling that of complete physical and nervous exhaustion.

John James Jones had once been a strikingly handsome fellow, with golden curly hair, a stalwart physique, square-jawed face, and long-lashed eyes of skylark-blue. The precise shade of blue, in fact, known to melt feminine reserve in the shortest span of time, and to elevate the emotions of women to the veritable melting-point.

But his experiences, it would seem, had reduced him to a gaunt skeleton of a man, with fear-haunted eyes and a feeble, trembling voice.

Under Zarkon's ministrations, the young American soon recovered from his swoon. Powerful restoratives returned him to a semblance of his former self. He was all too eager to tell the tale of his remarkable and horrifying adventures, and the narrative soon proved to be an astonishing one.

When the blond young man had quit his job in a rage over being accused of finagling Phoenicia Mulligan into marriage simply to get his hands on her fortune, he had come back to the islands determined to find his own. One lucky strike could repair his self-esteem, and would certainly improve his prospects. Perhaps even to such a point at which suspicious Braxton T. Crawley would no longer balk at giving his permission for the nuptials young Johnny Jones so ardently desired.

Why had he come back to Rangatoa, even after his own survey had shown the mineral deposits on the island, such as they were, to be thoroughly worthless from an industrial point of view? This was one of the questions Prince Zarkon addressed to the young man, as soon as he was able to talk.

"I don't know," murmured the boy. Then, setting his square jaw stubbornly, he added: "Guess I had to start somewhere . . . and it would really have been a feather in my cap to have dug up something of real worth, after Pacific Mining and Minerals had officially declared the island of no value, mineralogically speaking!"

"And did you find anything?" inquired Zarkon gently.

The boy reluctantly shook his head. "No, but it wasn't entirely my fault . . . and I'm still not convinced the island has no valuable metals," he declared.

"What do you mean, it wasn't entirely your fault? *What* wasn't your fault?" murmured the Man of Mysteries.

The blond boy shrugged helplessly. "I mean I never had a chance to finish up my survey—to do a really thorough job."

"And why not?"

The boy gestured weakly. "I dunno, Prince Zarkon—funny things started to happen—"

"What sort of things?"

"Like tools mislaid, or lost, or—stolen! Equipment that I couldn't easily replace. Things I know were there the day before, but were just plain *gone* the next day!"

"Petty pilferage, you mean," suggested the Lord of the Unknown.

"'Petty pilferage,' nothing! Nobody's going to carry off a twelve-thousand-electron-volt planar unit! Damned thing weighs half a ton. It'd take a pickup truck to move it . . . and why would anybody steal a planar unit in the first place? They couldn't get it off the island, and even if they did—what would they do with it? How could they dispose of it? Where could they possibly sell such a sophisticated piece of equipment?"

"What's a planar unit, Doc?" asked Scorchy in a hoarse

whisper. The big, dumb-looking man bent low to mutter in his ear.

"'S like a sonar set, Scorchy—probes for deposits of metals underground by subelectronic pulsations. You know how a radar wave bounces back off of any solid object?" whispered the man with the marvel mind.

"Unh-huh," grunted the runty little Irishman.

Doc Jenkins spread his baseball-mitt-size hands. "Well, planar waves only rebound from metal—and all other kinds of matter are not even there, as far as they are concerned. They go right through rock and sand and soil."

Scorchy indicated his comprehension with a nod. He started to ask something, then shut up, for Johnny Jones was talking again.

"I guess somebody—or some*thing*—was trying to discourage me, to scare me and get me to shut down my survey, get me away from the island," he muttered. "Well, I didn't budge! Then the two native workmen I had doing the spadework saw something up on the mountain. It scared them so badly they ran off the next day and never came back."

"I take it that they weren't local boys?" inquired Prince Zarkon.

Johnny shook his head. "No, they were a couple of geology students I hired on the main island. They were going to lend me a hand during vacations. Didn't matter so much, them running off when they did, 'cause they'd've had to go back anyway, once college opened again."

"So you were left alone?"

"Right. And then . . . *I saw it, myself!*"

Johnny's feeble, quavering tones sharpened with shrill fear: his wasted, worn features convulsed; his wide blue eyes were clouded with the shadow of horrible memories.

"Saw what?" demanded Zarkon, leaning closer. "*What did you see?*"

"I . . . I saw the volcano monster . . . coming up out of the crater . . . walking unharmed through live steam that would scald a man to death in minutes, wading through molten lava whose temperature was over one thousand degrees Fahrenheit . . . liquid rock so hot you can soften a steel bar by sticking it into the stuff . . . *and the ogre waded through it like it was tepid seawater!*"

The boy shuddered, plunging his face into his hands.

"It was *horrible*. Like a crude stone idol brought to life by some evil magician. It had no face, no eyes. But it could feel that I was there, and it came after me . . . red-hot and smoking, it climbed up out of the lava lake and came lumbering after me . . . ponderous, slow, dragging steps, like it weighed tons . . . and all the time, rivulets of molten lava were running down over its face and chest and shoulders—streams of liquid rock that would sear you or me to the bone in a tenth of a second . . . so I ran . . . into the swamp . . . and kept on running . . ."

His voice, weak and shaky, faded. His head lolled loosely on one shoulder, slack-jawed and empty-eyed. He had passed out again. But at least he had survived the ordeal without serious physical harm. Although he looked like a nervous wreck and would take some time to recuperate, at least the hapless young geologist had escaped alive from the burning death the volcano ogre had dealt to its other victims.

After some time, the Omega men, Phoenicia Mulligan, her uncle, and Señor Valdez emerged from the room in which John James Jones lay, asleep under heavy sedation administered by Prince Zarkon. They all looked tense, worried, distraught.

"Pore kid," rumbled Braxton T. Crawley through his huge set of mustachios. "Looks like he's sure gone through heck, back there. What a time he's had, hidin' out in the swamp, afraid t' come out f'r fear the volcano critter'd be lurkin' around his dang-fool cabin, waitin' for him . . . drinkin' muddy water, sleeping in a ditch, eatin' rotten fruit . . . 's a wonder he ain't half-dead, after a day er two of *thet!*"

"Yeah, cripes!" shivered Scorchy. "Here, allatime we wuz thinkin' him dead an' all—lissenin' t' his yarn is like havin' some poor soul come back from the grave t' tell ya what it's like onna other side."

Phoenicia Mulligan looked wan and troubled. "Poor Johnny's so frail and wasted-looking," she said faintly, "he looks like a walking corpse!" She shuddered, for the shades of night were falling, and island evenings were moist and downright cold during this season. "You wouldn't think a couple of days and nights in the swamps could wear down a man that way. He was always so strong and healthy!"

Braxton T. Crawley patted her shoulder clumsily.

"Why, sure, honey-chil'! Them swamps can do a white man in quicker'n quick—drinkin' thet dirty water, sleepin' in th' mud—fever—dysentery—leeches suckin' yer blood! But don't you worry, little gal. We'll get yer young man over to the mainland and a good hospital—"

"Señor Crawley," murmured the old hidalgo, "there is no need to worry. Over on the big island there is a first-rate modern hospital, fully staffed and equipped to deal with island fevers."

"Yeah, by golly, that's right," rumbled the fat little man in his bullfrog voice. "Savage Memorial Hospital, right? Heerd of the place myself. So don't you go a-worryin'—we'll see the young feller gets well again!"

Phoenicia Mulligan blinked back tears, sniffed loudly, and peered with misty eyes at her avuncular relation.

"B-but, Uncle B-Braxton, I th-thought you didn't *like* Johnny! You s-said he was just a fuf-fortune-hunter!"

"Well. *Hrrmph!*" snorted the fat man shame-facedly. "Just you ne'mine what I said. Guess I sorta misjudged the young feller . . . now I got me a chance t' make up f'r figgerin' him wrong th' fust time around."

"Yes, I wouldn't worry, miss," drawled Nick Naldini comfortingly. "Our chief's got a degree in medicine and is reckoned a brilliant physician. Bet you he can fix the boy up good as new! Chances are he just needs a good stiff dose o' quinine and a few days' bed-rest and some good food in him. In no time he'll be up and around, good as new—"

"I'm afraid not," said a quiet voice from behind them, as soon as Phoenicia Mulligan had said her goodnights and gone off to bed. They turned as Zarkon emerged from the shadows of the doorway.

"How's the kid, chief?" inquired Menlo Parker brightly. The skinny little scientist usually maintained a glum-faced, sour-eyed silence when women were around, but cheered up quick as a flash once the pretty creatures were out of sight. Old Menlo was such a confirmed and devout misogynist that his comrades on the Omega team often jokingly suggested he had a physical allergy to silk stockings and soprano voices.

"Not good," said Zarkon in a serious voice. "We'd better get him to the big hospital on the main island. But right now I don't want him moved. He's quite ill; his experience has taken a heavy toll."

"Aw, shucks, the poor kid," grumbled Scorchy. "Well, we'll sic Fooey Mulligan on him t'morra for a nurse. With a blond cutie like that t' hold yer hand and stick a thermometer in yer kisser, it's almost worthwhile bein' sick!"

"So what d'we do now, chief? Call it a day and turn in?" inquired Ace Harrigan. The handsome aviator looked glum. He thought he was getting places fast with the gorgeous young heiress, but now that her boy-friend had turned up alive after all, his chances looked about nil.

Zarkon suggested that they all get a good night's sleep. Then, pausing by the window of the room where poor John James Jones lay sleeping under a heavy dose of sedative, the Ultimate Man looked grim.

"Best we all get some sleep now," he said firmly. "With dawn tomorrow I mean to descend into the crater of Mount Rangatoa—"

Nick licked his lips. "Chief, you can't go down in that devil's soup-pot! Not even an insulated suit c'd keep a man alive in that hellish brew!"

Zarkon shook his head determinedly.

"I came prepared, Nick. I packed along in the equipment cases a new experimental heat suit. The new plastic boron-fiber insulation should prove sufficient, even against molten lava. I am confident of it, at any rate."

"What the heck you gonna do down inside the volcano?" demanded Scorchy curiously.

"Find the secret lair of the fire-devil," said Zarkon. "Or try to, anyway!"

CHAPTER 11

It Walks by Night

Night fell, purple-winged, across the calm waters of the Pacific. As the sun died gorgeously on the western horizon, one by one the first few timid stars ventured forth. First only a few; then dozens shone and twinkled.

The purple vault deepened to black velvet. Now the stars blazed and shimmered in numberless legions, turning the night sky to a jeweler's display. Like heaped and scattered ice-blue diamonds, the innumerable constellations of the tropic sky displayed their dazzling splendors.

The small village of Tarapaho slumbered beneath the starry blaze. In their thatched huts, the native fishermen and farmers slept beside their women and children. They were raised a little off the ground on pilings, those huts. Chickens huddled together, clucking sleepily from time to time, under the porches. Bony-ribbed dogs whimpered and kicked in the alleys between the huts, dreaming their doggy dreams of running, hunting, eating.

In all the village, nothing stirred.

But within the black depths of the jungle, a strange, hulking shape was on the prowl.

It lumbered clumsily, on heavy, stumpy feet, crackling through the underbrush. From time to time it paused, its massive, neckless head turned a little to one side, as if listening. It had no face, that head—no eyes or ears. But somehow it seemed to be listening, to be snuffling the air, to see if its approach was noticed.

In the sleeping village, nothing moved or walked or seemed aware that hulking horror lurked monstrously within the jungle aisles. Only one or two of the starveling dogs whined in their sleep, wrinkling their pointed noses, scenting on the breeze the approach of the monster.

It had not the smell of living flesh. Instead, it smelled of burnt rock. The dogs sneezed, rolled over, began to snooze and dream again.

The huge shape appeared at the jungle's edge.

It peered this way and that, up and down the length of the village street.

At the end of this street, with its back up against the volcano, stood the trading-post of Señor Valdez. It was a large, rambling structure—the largest and most imposing of the buildings which composed the little village of Tarapaho.

Therein slept Phoenicia Mulligan and Braxton T. Crawley, the Omega men, and Señor Valdez himself.

A monstrous, hulking shape in the darkness, the ogre began to move with slow, dragging steps towards the trading-post. It kept just within the edge of the jungle, as if it feared to expose its hideousness to the pure light of the clear, luminous moon. Brush crackled and leaves rustled as the monstrous thing moved slowly through the bushes.

The rear wall of Señor Valdez' trading-post was built smack up against the slope of the mountain. The beginnings of the rocky incline angled beneath the flooring of the back of the building, where the storerooms were. The monster lumbered heavily through the shadows, pausing from time to time, its huge, featureless head lifted, questing from side to side, as though listening.

Then, satisfied that none had observed it, it stepped into the black gloom between the pilings on which the rear of the building was raised, and vanished into the darkness.

Slowly, feeling its way step by step, the weird figure strode underneath the platform on which the trading-post of Señor Valdez was built.

When it had reached the back end of the building, where the rocky ground began to rise on an inclined plane, it reached up, fumbling with thick paws at the flooring. The heavy boards creaked as the huge paws tested them one by one. Eventually the black shape in the shadows found one that was looser than the rest. Monstrous paws closed about one end of this board, tugging and twisting. With a squeak of nails torn loose, the board gave way.

The next board came loose easier and more silently than had the first. Before long the bulky shape had made an opening in the floor large enough to accommodate its girth.

Bracing its stumpy feet against the inclined plane of rock, and reaching up to grab hold of the edges of the opening it had made, the ogre climbed clumsily into the storeroom and was lost to view.

Oblivious to what had come prowling from the blackness of the jungle night, the village slept on.

Even the slumber of the bony-ribbed village hounds was undisturbed. Had the massive, slow-moving intruder smelled to their sensitive nostrils like a living creature, the wary mutts might have roused the sleeping villagers with their nervous yapping.

But, living in such close proximity to the volcanic

mountain, they were used to the smell of burnt rock, and paid no heed to a whiff of the odor of such fire-scorched stone.

Even when it walked like a man . . .

It was Phoenicia Mulligan who smelled it first. The hot smoke of burning wood and rattan matting, that is.

Worried sick on the behalf of her fiancé, John James Jones, the blond girl had slept but poorly, for all her nervous exhaustion. She had tossed and turned all night, rousing from time to time to pummel the lumpy pillow into a more amenable shape with her fists.

Then she smelled the smoke.

At first the blond girl ignored the acrid odor. Probably, she dismissed it as the last fumes from the feast cookfires, whose coals still glowed dimly in the darkness of the tropic night. The sleepy girl told herself that the smoke fumes were being brought inland on the breeze that blew from the lagoon.

Eventually the scent of smoke became too strong and choking for the distraught girl to ignore any longer, even though she wished to, for at last she was drifting off to sleep.

She sat up in bed and sniffed the air.

No doubt about it, it was smoke. Thick, pungent, choking, the fumes were filling the room. By the moonlight which streamed in through the bamboo slats covering the window, she could even see the stuff coiling on the air and collecting in layers.

Her pulses thudding with alarm, Fooey Mulligan jumped up, pulled on a dressing-robe over her flimsy nightgown of nylon tricot, and jerked open the door to her room.

The hall outside should have been pitch-black. But it

was not. A dim, wavering glow diffused orange light through the gloom. The light was filtering under the door at the end of the hall. That door, she vaguely remembered, led to the storage rooms where Señor Valdez kept his merchandise which had not yet been unpacked and placed on shelf display.

She went down the hall, curious. Perhaps the gentlemanly old Spaniard was conducting inventory, she postulated to herself, and the wavering orange glow, as well as the pungent fumes of smoke, came from a kerosene lamp.

Before she made a fool of herself before Prince Zarkon, by hysterically giving a false alarm, the girl decided to investigate.

She flung open the door to the storeroom, which was not latched.

Then she saw that the room was filled with black smoke, underlit by the licking orange flames.

Then she screamed!

Zarkon was at her side in moments. Oddly enough, although she did not really notice it at the time, the Lord of the Unknown was fully dressed in his gunmetal-gray slacks, pullover, and suede jacket and shoes.

The Ultimate Man took one look into the burning room, then jerked her about and propelled her back out into the hall with an ungentle push.

"Wake up the others!" he ordered. Then, slipping off his jacket and wrapping it loosely about his face and head, Zarkon plunged into the flames.

For a moment the bewildered girl hesitated. Then she went to the nearest door and rapped on it with frantic knuckles, calling loudly.

It opened and the silver-haired old hidalgo peered out,

blinking the sleep from his eyes. He needed no words from the young woman to comprehend the situation, for the hall was filled with drifting plumes of smoke and redly alit by the light of the flames.

Scorchy, Nick, and Ace shared the next room between them. They came popping out in various stages of undress, clutching their pistols. In a few moments Menlo Parker and Doc Jenkins joined them, as did Señor Valdez' old housekeeper, Maria, who began screaming hysterically at one glimpse of the licking flames.

"Get her outa here, willya?" demanded Scorchy urgently. "Rouse the villagers—"

"Yes! The alarm bell—on the veranda!" gasped the old Spaniard, gesticulating violently. Nodding crisply, Fooey Mulligan spun the old woman around and led her out onto the porch. She had noticed the old-fashioned iron bell which hung there when they had drunk tea on the veranda during the first afternoon on the island. Señor Valdez had explained to her that it was rung for emergencies, and that ringing it would summon the village menfolk.

Snatching up the iron doorstop, Fooey Mulligan beat the bell with it. The clangor was deafening. In no time tousled heads came popping out of huts, staring wild-eyed down the length of the village street to the trading-post at its terminus.

"Fire! *Fire!*" yelled the blond girl, wishing she could remember what the word was in Spanish. But either the villagers understood her meaning without translation or the smoke was clearly visible in the moonlight as it came boiling out through the cracks in the thatched roof of the trading-post. For in no time at all the villagers came out of the doors of their huts, hastily wrapping sarong-like lengths of cloth around their waists, to come pelting down the street towards the burning building.

One of them helped the hysterical Maria down the steps, while the others formed a line to the beach. Wooden buckets and empty gasoline tins appeared. These were hastily dipped into the calm waters of the lagoon and were passed, sloshing, from hand to hand along the length of the street, right up to the walls of the trading-post, where the village women and children gathered in a crowd to empty the buckets against the smoking walls.

Phoenicia Mulligan had heard of such "bucket brigades" before but had never chanced to see one in action. She found the sight fascinating. She was impressed by the instinctive way the villagers organized the thing without milling confusion or shouted orders. They seemed to know what to do automatically.

It never occurred to the fascinated blond girl that the natives of Rangatoa had probably been fighting fires in precisely this same manner from the dawn of time—or, at least, from whatever period of the past in which the volcanic island had first become settled.

So she got out of the way of the men and watched as the most primitive method of firefighting was demonstrated in action.

Several boys even climbed up on the roof to douse down the smoking thatch with buckets of water passed up to them. As the flames touched the wet roof, the smoke turned vile and poisonously black, the boys retreated, coughing and gagging, unable to breathe the sooty stuff.

Scorchy and Nick Naldini emerged from the burning building, loaded with gear. The two presented an unconsciously comical appearance, both clad only in their shorts. While the pint-sized boxer had a well-developed physique, in miniature, as it were, the lanky stage magician was all skin and bones by comparison. All dressed up in his usual natty finery, the Mephistophelian magician looked sardonic and impressive: seen in his skivvies, he presented a rather ludicrous appearance, especially when the muscular bantamweight boxer stood beside him, similarly stripped for action.

After them, Braxton T. Crawley and Señor Valdez came stumbling out into the open, followed by Ace Harrigan, Menlo Parker, and Doc Jenkins. Prince Zarkon was nowhere to be seen.

Suddenly the blond girl uttered a piercing shriek and clapped her hands to her face guiltily.

"You okay, toots?" panted Scorchy.

"*Johnny!*" the girl shrilled. "I forgot to knock on *his* door!" The fact that the room occupied by the sick young geologist was on the farther side of the building, and did not have a door which opened onto the central hall, as did all the ones on whose doors she had pounded in order to rouse their sleeping occupants, did nothing to alleviate the guilty feelings the girl suffered.

"Cheez," gasped the little Irish boxer. "And the chief knocked him out with a heavy dose o' sedative, too! Th' poor gink's slept through the whole thing! Well," he gritted determinedly, "here goes nuttin'!"

"What are you g-going to d-do?" wailed the girl in alarm.

Scorchy snatched one of the buckets as it was being passed from hand to hand down the firefighting line, and up-ended it, dousing himself with cold lagoon-water from head to foot.

"Gotta git th' poor guy outa there," growled the pugnacious Pride of the Muldoons through chattering teeth.

And before either Nick Naldini or Phoenicia Mulligan could think to move or speak a word to stop him, the midget prizefighter sprang up the stairs to the veranda porch, plunged into the open doorway, and vanished in the boiling clouds of smoke.

CHAPTER 12

The Murder Monster

Only a few moments after Scorchy Muldoon plunged into the smoke-filled doorway of the burning building and disappeared, a black shape came around the porch of the veranda, with a gaunt burden in its arms.

It was Prince Zarkon, his face and clothing black with soot and smeared ash, bearing the half conscious, feebly-struggling body of John James Jones.

The Omega Man jumped down the steps, depositing the limp figure of the ill geologist on the dewy grass. Then he began slapping sparks from the smoldering scorched places in his clothing.

"Is he all right?" inquired Phoenicia Mulligan in an anxious voice.

Zarkon bent to examine the famished figure, whose bony face gleamed with perspiration and was smeared and dirty from smoke and soot. Then he nodded.

"I found him on the ground underneath the window to his room," said the Man of Mysteries.

"Gosh," exclaimed Nick Naldini worriedly. "We figgered th' poor guy'd still be knocked out from the drugs you gave him last night, chief, and'd be overcome by smoke by this time!"

"He musta choked an' coughed himse'f awake, when

the smoke got thick enough," rumbled Braxton T. Crawley in his deep voice. "An' managed to climb er fall outa his window! Pore feller! Shore din't do him much good, in his sick condition! Quicker we c'n git him to a hospital on the main island, th' better for my future nephew-in-law!"

"Oh, Uncle Braxton!" squealed Phoenicia Mulligan ecstatically, "does that mean what it sounds like? You'll let me and Johnny get married, after all, with no objections?"

The fat man flushed scarlet, scowling ferociously as his happy niece twined her arms around his neck and gave him a resounding kiss on one plump cheek.

"Well, heck," grumbled the industrialist, blowing out his walrus mustache with a snort. "After all this young feller's been through, I'd be an ogre myself, t' stand in the way o' you youngsters any longer."

The girl kissed him again, grinning blissfully.

"Speakin' of ogres, chief," hailed Ace Harrigan, coming up to join the group gathered around the recumbent figure of the young geologist under the trees, "guess what started the fire?"

"The appropriately named 'fire-devil,' I gather from your tone," commented Zarkon with a slight smile.

The handsome aviator nodded vigorously. "Right as rain, chief! Señor Valdez and me, we went under the house to scout around. Found where the thing broke in, out in back, by ripping away part of the floor."

"You sure it was the ogre, not just some human firebug?" inquired Menlo Parker suspiciously.

Ace Harrigan nodded. "No doubt about it," the aviator said positively. "Found one of the thing's footprints in the dirt on top of the rocks, where it braced itself t' climb in through the hole it had made in the floor. Footprint like an elephant or a rhino or something, no toe-marks or claw-scratches or anything, just a big thick pad-like print.

It was the monster, all right! The touch of its red-hot hands or body musta set fire to the stuff in the storeroom—"

"Why, thet murderin' critter!" wheezed Braxton T. Crawley, puffing with indignation. "Dang-fool thing, it tried to burn us in our beds!"

Zarkon looked grim. His lips parted to give voice to some remark, but, as things turned out, his words never got spoken. For suddenly Nick Naldini, stung by something the fat industrialist had just said, jumped guiltily and cried out.

"'Burn us in our beds'?" he croaked in alarm. "Cripes, that reminds me! Holy Houdini, chief—*Scorchy just ran back inside there to get Johnny Jones out!* We figgered as how he'd still be knocked out from the sedative you gave 'im! *And Scorchy ain't come out yet!*"

Instinctively, all eyes turned to the burning building. By now it was a raging inferno. Flames roared from every window; oily black smoke gushed from the interstices between the boards of the walls and leaked thinly through the wet thatched roof. The interior of the doomed building was one solid mass of seething, white-hot flame, like the inside of a furnace.

Zarkon froze motionless for a split second, and across his face there came an expression of horror and dread such as none of them had ever before seen distort his features.

Seldom did the Man from Tomorrow register emotion. Most of the time he maintained an expressionless mask of serenity. But emotion was there now, rawly visible in his horror-struck eyes.

Only one thing could stir fear or horror within Zarkon. And that was the thought of serious harm or the death of one of the five men who fought by his side in his great crusade against evil. The five men who had leagued with him in the cause of Omega were the only human beings close to him in this age, his only friends. His love for his comrades was evident now in the horror that rose within him at the thought of one of them alone in that raging holocaust.

Then, in the next instant, Zarkon was on his feet and running for the burning building.

And at his side was Nick Naldini. The expression of horror had vanished from the features of the Lord of the Unknown by this time, for he had regained his self-control.

But fear was written large in the long horse-face of the vaudevillian. Although he would rather have died than have let Scorchy realize the depth of his feelings, the lanky magician was horrified at the thought of Scorchy's danger. Ostensibly the bitterest of feuding foes, the two men were like brothers, although each would have perished from shame rather than let the other know how he felt.

"How's about one a you birds helpin' me down from up here," came a familiar voice from above their heads.

Nick Naldini stopped short, as if he had just run into an invisible wall. Craning his neck, the stage magician stared up at the smoking thatched roof of the burning building. There, seated gingerly on the edge, was the soot-black figure of Scorchy Muldoon.

"Scorchy, are you all right?" inquired Prince Zarkon.

"All right?" coughed the little boxer indignantly. "Sure 'n Oi've inhaled enough smoke t' make me swear off cigarettes fer life, Oi have! Dunno where Johnny Jones is, chief, but he sure ain't in his room, at all, at all. *Ouch*, this blamed roof is gettin' so hot it's blisterin' me backside! If any o' you goggle-eyed goons c'd just leave off starin' at a feller fer long enough t' git 'im down from here, Oi'd be that obliged, Oi would!"

It was dawn before they could make any serious estimate of the damage. Surprisingly enough, it turned out to be superficial, after all. While the entire rear of the trading-post had been completely gutted, and the storeroom, pantry, and kitchen were totally destroyed by the fire, the remainder of the rooms and the building itself still stood and were relatively unharmed.

The only way to account for this was the simple fact that the structure and flooring were made of hard island woods, like teak logs, and the walls dividing the building into rooms were made mostly of hollow bamboo tubes. Few woods are harder than teak, and bamboo, because of its slick, glossy outer sheath, is remarkably difficult to set afire. Once the conflagration had been drowned, and the smoke aired out, the rest of the building was in pretty fair shape, although black and foul with soot and dirty water, and charred in many places.

At the last minute, what saved the building from being completely gutted was the unexpected arrival of outside help. The native firefighters with their primitive bucket-brigade had been instrumental in halting the spread of the flames, but what really turned the trick was the landing of the sailors from the crew of Fooey Mulligan's yacht, the *Phoenicia*, which was anchored offshore near the rocketplane in which the Omega men had come to the island.

The crew of the yacht had been asleep, except for the duty officer and the deck-watch. It had taken them some time to notice the flames, for at first the rising plumes of smoke had been mistaken for vapor coming from the volcano itself. Once Phoenicia Mulligan's sailors had realized their natural mistake, however, the sailors had come swiftly to the aid of the villagers, with sophisticated firefighting equipment of the sort that smothers flames beneath a thick, sudsy layer of chemical foam.

When the full damage to the trading-post had been estimated, which was not until morning when they could explore the char-blackened interior by light of day, the destruction caused by the fire proved trivial enough, and less than they might have imagined.

Señor Valdez even managed to be quite cheerful about it. His friends among the workmen of the village could easily enough repair the damage, he said, and as for the loss of his surplus stock, well, his supplies had been rather low at the time and could quickly be replenished when the next boat came from the main island, where he placed his orders.

"It is indeed fortunate that I have done well in my business over the years," said the gentlemanly old hidalgo, "and have managed to place many pesos on deposit in the vaults of the First National Bank of Mantilla. One must, somehow, remain philosophical in the face of adversity and of calamities such as this one! Merchandise can be replaced; but I give my thanks that in the fire naught was destroyed but goods. Human lives cannot be replaced," he said, crossing himself fervently. "I would be irreparably injured had any of my distinguished guests been harmed by the conflagration while visiting under my roof!"

Scorchy thought that the old man's sentiments were eminently admirable. He could not understand why Nick Naldini scowled so satanically when the silver-haired gentleman expressed them in his eloquent, Old-World manner.

"What's eatin' *you*, Long, Lean, and Ugly?" he

demanded in a scornful whisper. "Seems t' me th' old geezer's bein' pretty nice about it!"

"I'm not denying that, Short and Stupid," his friend snorted contemptuously. "I guess you're just too thick-witted to have thought about *what else* was burned up in that fire besides a mess of canned goods!"

Scorchy scratched his slightly-singed scalp puzzledly.

"I don't get yer meanin', me bucko," he confessed.

"Our equipment cases, you cretin!" hissed Nick Naldini under his breath. "We stored all the equipment cases we brought with us in that storeroom! They were completely destroyed in the fire, they and their contents, too!"

"Yeah, well, so what?" grunted Scorchy unconcernedly. "We ain't needed 'em yet, and we got some back-up gadgets out in the tail storage-compartment of the *Skyrocket*, and the chief's rich enough t' replace all the lost equipment and never feel it. So what's eatin' you?"

Nick gritted his teeth, squeezed his fists tightly, and tried to be calm.

"It hasn't occurred to you, then, Small Change," he snarled sarcastically, "that packed away in those cases was an experimental heatproof suit the chief was gonna use this morning to go down inside the volcano and see if he could find the place the fire-devil hides out, when he isn't out rampagin' through the countryside, killin' folks and settin' fire to things?"

Scorchy's eyes popped. He voiced a low whistle.

"Jeez, that's right, Nick," muttered the runty boxer. "I fergot about the heat-suit, what with all the excitement around here—"

"What's more," hissed the lanky vaudeville artist venomously, "just last night, when we were going to bed, the chief announced his intentions of using the special suit to git down inside the mountain—in front of us all! He was standing right in out on the veranda when he said it."

"That's right," mused Scorchy thoughtfully, scratching his bestubbled chin with one thumbnail. "Even John James Jones coulda heard 'im, if'n he was still awake then, 'cause the chief was standing right under the open window to his room—"

"Yeah," remarked Nick with a leering grin, "*—and so could anyone . . . or anything . . . that might-a been lurkin' around the edge of the woods, listenin' and tryin' t' overhear our plans!*"

Scorchy shivered nervously and shot an anxious glance into the thick wall of vegetation that edged the clearing in which the village was built.

"You mean you think the volcano monster was hangin' around, out there somewhere, and heard the chief talkin' about the heat-suit?" he demanded feebly.

"That's exactly what I think," snapped Nick Naldini.

Scorchy sneaked another surreptitious glance at the silent mass of palm-trees and thick, motionless bushes. Then he shivered again—and not just because he was still standing around in nothing but his shorts.

CHAPTER 13

Introducing Chicago Louie

After a hasty breakfast, Prince Zarkon and the five lieutenants took the skiff out to where the *Skyrocket* was anchored in the bay. Nick and Doc and Scorchy had wearied of running around in nothing but their shorts, and if there was going to be any mountain-climbing to do, they wanted to be suitably dressed for the occasion.

Luckily, the lockers aboard the experimental rocket-plane contained spare clothing for them all, including the Man of Mysteries, whose gunmetal gray jacket, slacks, and turtle-neck pullover were considerably the worse for wear, after his experiences in the blazing trading-post the night before.

While they climbed into fresh clothes, Scorchy queried the Ultimate Man on the course of their investigations.

"Say, chief, now that this heat-suit of yours was ruined in the fire, along with everything else in the equipment cases, how we gonna get down inside of that dang volcano?" he asked inquiringly. "Now that I got some fresh duds on, I don't exactly relish the thought o' gettin' 'em burnt off'n me by goin' skinny-dippin' in a lake a lava!"

"I wouldn't worry about that if I were you, Scorchy," replied Zarkon gravely. "Without the heat-suit, I'm afraid it will be impossible for us to investigate the interior of the volcano crater at first hand."

"So that's out, eh, chief?" piped Doc Jenkins cheerfully. It was noticed by his comrades that the huge, dumb-looking man with the miracle brain did not exactly sound depressed or woeful over the news that the expedition down into the interior of Mount Rangatoa had been called off.

The fact of the matter was that Doc was not exactly enamored of the notion of climbing mountains. "Everest-or-Bust!" was a motto that could never, by any stretch of the imagination, be ascribed to the big, clumsy man with the outsized hands and feet. It was not so much that Theophilus "Doc" Jenkins suffered from acrophobia, or fear of heights, as it was that, like many big men, he was clumsy, and like many clumsy men, when nervous he tended to exaggerate his inclination to stumble over his own feet.

Doc had been known to trip and stumble over a postage stamp pasted to a mirror-smooth ballroom floor. Or so Menlo Parker claimed, anyway, it being the skinny little scientist's chief pleasure in life to good-humoredly rag his lumbering, heavy-footed colleague over his propensities to trip over his own outsized dogs. Given this tendency to exaggerate his own clumsiness, though, it's easy enough to see why the fine art of mountain-climbing was not exactly Doc's notion of a fun thing to do.

"Doc don't sound too crushed over the idee of not climbin' around inside the volcano, does he?" grinned Menlo with a nasty cackle.

"He sure doesn't," laughed Ace. "Big lummox probably figures if he has to climb the thing, he'll probably fall off down the other side."

Menlo emitted another cackle. "If that much beef ever fell off th' mountain," he smirked, with an ogle at Doc's huge torso, "it'd bounce from here t' Cleveland!"

Flushing scarlet, Doc said plaintively, "Now, lissen here, you skinny old beanstalk, you! You watch yer tongue —it ain't nice ta keep on alla time makin' cracks about a feller's size 'n' weight 'n'—"

"—And remarkable talent for falling over a dime flat on his big puss, eh?" sneered the little man, dancing nimbly out of the way as Doc made a halfhearted grab for him.

"Lay off, you two," grinned Scorchy. "Nick an' I, we got the local feudin' concession in *this* here gang!"

While the Omega men repaired to their plane for a change of clothing, Miss Phoenicia Mulligan had her sailors take her and her uncle out to the yacht to replenish their own missing haberdashery. Fooey Mulligan, who, despite her adventuresome inclinations, was all gal deep down where it mattered in the instincts, kept her closets aboard the *Phoenicia* well-stuffed with the latest creations of Park Avenue and Paris. In no time she was fully rigged and ready to sail.

Locating a change of clothes for Braxton T. Crawley, however, proved quite a problem. The red-faced industrialist with the walrus mustache was so fat that he was twice the size of even the heftiest seaman aboard the *Phoenicia*. Fussing and fuming, the fat man struggled to squeeze his rotund girth into a variety of clothes his niece's crew obligingly dug up for him from sea-chest and ship's locker, but to no avail. The sailors themselves got a good laugh out of the spectacle.

"Gee, you'd sure make a good sailor, Mr. Crawley," said one young crewman with a straight face.

"I would, eh?" puffed the fat man, ruefully regarding a pair of dungarees whose every seam he had just split asunder. "How come, young feller?"

Another seaman lounging nearby guffawed loudly.

"What Red means, Mr. Crawley," he grinned, cocking a thumb at the fat man's belly, "you'd never hafta worry about bein' swep' overboard in a storm. Ya sorta got a built-in life preserver, if ya know what I mean—"

"Is that so, you young whippersnapper," growled the fat man with a glare that would have stopped any self-respecting torpedo dead in its tracks at thirty yards. "Well, let me tell you something, you dang-fool better be glad you work for my niece Fooey an' not for me, or you'd be down pumpin' out the hatches and battenin' down the bilge for the rest o' this here voyage!"

Fooey Mulligan thrust her blond head in the cabin door, looking remarkably smart in white ducks and a blue pullover.

"Uncle Braxton, will you stop badgering my men, and shake a leg?" she suggested sharply. "And you mean 'battening down the *hatches* and pumping out the *bilge,'*" she added by way of an afterthought.

"Hesh up!" rumbled her uncle flusteredly. "I sure dang-fool know what I dang-fool mean! And these-here sailor-boys of your'n are badgerin' *me!* Git busy and find me some clo'es t' fit a full-grown man, willya?"

Eventually, from a fat Chinese cook, Braxton T. Crawley found trousers and a striped jersey almost large enough to squeeze into, and after Phoenicia let out a seam or two—or maybe three—with a lot of pushing and groaning and jamming and squeezing they got the fat man dressed and into the skiff.

On the beach it was Scorchy who first spotted Fooey Mulligan in her nautical threads. The little boxer, always highly susceptible where blondes were concerned (not to mention brunettes and redheads), popped his eyes and let his jaw hang loose at the sight she made in the tight slacks and even tighter pullover.

"Wowie," he said faintly.

"Close your yap, Irish, before you start catching flies," snapped the girl.

"Yes'm," he breathed. "Wowie."

"Wowie to you, and plenty of 'em," the girl said feelingly. "Where's the action?"

"Down at Señor Valdez' trading-post," said Scorchy with a sappy expression on his face. "W—"

"I know. Wowie," said Phoenicia Mulligan, heading for the burnt building.

"Where you been hiding, Short an' Ugly?" inquired Nick Naldini amiably, strolling up to where Scorchy stood transfixed as if suddenly rooted to the spot, a glassy look in his eyes.

When his query elicited no response, Nick peered more closely at his Hibernian comrade, waved one languid hand in front of the fixed and staring eyes, then pinched his arm fiercely. Scorchy jumped, bleated, and rubbed his arm, giving the lanky vaudevillian an accusing glower.

"Thought rigor mortis had set in," drawled Nick, looking relieved. "What's up? Gettin' the glad-eye from the local hula-hula gal?"

"Fooey Mulligan," said Scorchy fervently. "Wait'll ya see her! She fills up a tight pair o' white ducks like nothin' you ever saw. Doesn't look half bad in a tight pullover, either!" he added, smacking his lips.

Nick groaned and rolled his eyes. As Scorchy stalked off in pursuit of the blonde, who by now had reached the farther end of the village street, where Señor Valdez' trading-post stood, Nick turned to Braxton T. Crawley, who had come waddling up, wheezing uncomfortably in his straining trousers.

"Never fails," moaned Nick, shaking his head.

"Huh? Whuzzat?" grumbled the fat man.

Nick cocked a thumb at the retreating Irishman. "Pint-size, there. If there's a cute dish in one of these capers of ours, and there usually is, ol' Thyroid Deficiency there falls all over himself tryin' to make out like it was high-school graduation night and his regiment leaves at dawn. Gal always and invariably goes ga-ga over the chief and gives our Son o' the Emerald Isle the cold shoulder."

"Eh? My niece, you mean? Well, well," chuckled Braxton T. Crawley happily. "Attracted the eye of your Irish friend, has she? Do her a world of good. Just what thet dang-fool niece of mine needs! Meet a good man, get married up, settle down, have a flock o' kids, and git all this hair-brained rushing around the world havin' adventures out o' her system!"

Nick's mouth fell open. "D'you mean you'd *encourage* this mésalliance?" he demanded incredulously. But Crawley had waddled off, humming the Wedding March.

When Nick Naldini joined his friends before the trading-post, he found quite a crowd gathered there.

"What's happening?" he asked.

Ace Harrigan looked around, grinning. "Visitors from the big island," chuckled the handsome aviator. "One of 'em's the local cop for this part of the islands—wait'll you meet him! 'Chicago Louie,' Menlo calls this one."

The crowd parted, making way for a remarkable little man who strode up to eye Nick from toe to crown with a gleaming, knowing glint in his eye. This apparition wore plainclothes: a suit with a loud check and wide lapels, and a snap-brimmed fedora pulled down over one glittering eye. Pointy-toe shoes of alligator-hide with elevator heels adorned his small feet. He was remarkably ugly, with a swarthy complexion, greasy skin, a straggly black mustache, and a leering, snaggle-toothy grin, wherein handfuls of gold fillings flashed and twinkled. His pop-eyes looked like two boiled eggs. The general impression he gave was of a racetrack tout dressed for a weekend in Las Vegas.

Señor Valdez accompanied him, and began to introduce Nick Naldini in Spanish; but the grotesque little man in the garish tweeds cut him off imperiously.

"Hi spik the Ingleesh vairy goodly-enough, t'anks," he snorted. "No need to *habla Espagnol* wiv me, señor. An' thees," he said, fixing Nick with a goggling eye, "thees ees Señor Neekolouz Naldeeni, ees eet?"

"Eet ees," said Nick. "I mean, *it is!*"

"Ho-ho," the odd-looking little man chuckled for some reason, rocking back and forth teeteringly on his heels. While the elevator heels added considerably to his height, the little Spanish cop only came up to Nick's armpits.

Suddenly leaning close, giving Nick a whiff of an overpowering cologne strong enough to drive off famished timber wolves, the little man whispered hoarsely: "Do you know H*om*phrey Bogart?"

"Humphrey Bogart," murmured Nick blankly.

The little man waggled his head delightedly. "Hyess! H*om*phrey Bogart ees my, how you say, my hidol!" he confided with a disconcerting giggle. "H'always he ees a priwate eye—"

"A *what?*"

"A *priwate eye,* fighteeng crooks een Chicago. *Hai, caramba,*" sighed the comical little dwarf, "how Hi would laav to be a priwate eye! Seexteen times Hi 'ave seen *The Malteez Fawcon! Seexteen times.* 'Ave hyou seen *The Malteez Fawcon?*"

"Yeah," mumbled Nick.

"*Hai, caramba!* He ees a shrewd one, that Sam Spade . . . maybe, when Hi reetire, how you say, I go to

Chicago an' meet H*om*phrey Bogart an' beecom' a priwate eye . . . another Sam Spade, how you say?"

"Yeah," mumbled Nick.

Zarkon emerged from the grinning crowd.

"Nick, this is Señor Luis Gonzalez of the Luzon Islands Constabulary Force, here to assist us in our investigation of the volcano-ogre murders."

"Yeah," mumbled Nick. "Just what we need. A little help."

CHAPTER 14

The Island Hawkshaw

It would seem that Señor Luis Gonzalez, dissatisfied by the report of the original and rather cursory investigation into the murder of Tommy Kahua and Jimmie Okawa, had decided to take a personal look into the case. If possible, the grotesque little island Sherlock hoped to come up with the solution to the mystery himself.

At the very least, he could hardly do less than the Luzon police had done. His goggling eyes agleam, the little man in the loud checked suit decided to emulate his fictional hero, Raymond Chandler's famous Sam Spade, and scout around on his own.

The first person Luis Gonzalez encountered in the village was Phoenicia Mulligan. The attractive blond girl was one of the principals in this mystery which he had yet to interrogate. She was also remarkably pretty. So Luis Gonzalez thrust himself into her path.

"'Allo, switthot," he growled out of the side of his mouth. It was just the sort of thing Humphrey Bogart always said to the women in his movies. It was not the fault of Luiz Gonzalez that his accent was so thick that the remark came out sounding nothing at all like the deadpan voice of his favorite movie idol.

The girl looked him up and down, repressing a grin.

The astounding suit, such as had not been worn by mortal man for thirty years, except in period movies, fascinated her.

"Hello, Señor Gonzalez." She smiled, having heard all about the detective's comical ways from Nick and Scorchy. "Hot on the trail of Sidney Greenstreet, are you? Or is it Peter Lorre?"

Luis Gonzalez grinned toothily, displaying enough gold to make the officials at Fort Knox hurriedly count their stock, just in case. The little detective did not particularly mind being kidded about his fascination for "priwate eye" pictures. He was good-humored about it.

"'Ave hyou evair meet H*om*phrey Bogart?" he inquired.

The girl laughed. "No, can't say that I have! I did meet Lauren Bacall once, at a charity dinner, though," she recollected.

The Hispanic Sherlock looked puzzled.

"Who?"

"Lauren Bacall. You know—Mr. Bogart's wife."

He glowered up at the tall blonde, a distrustful expression visible on his ugly features.

"H*om*phrey Bogart," he informed her in a hurt tone of voice, "ees married to Maria Astor. Aftair she sairved time in the beeg house, that ees!"

"Okay," said Fooey Mulligan cheerfully, willing to go along with Luis Gonzalez' private version of events. "I stand corrected."

"What do hyou know about thees murders?" the dwarfed detective inquired sharply, regarding the blond girl with a suspicious eye. Obviously, in his book, anyone so ill-informed on the subject of his movie hero was not to be trusted.

"Not much," the girl cracked. "What do *you* know about 'em?"

The little cop winked cunningly. "Thair ees more afoot than meets the heye," he said in a conspiratorial whisper. "A clevair hand ees behind thees crimes. But he 'ad bettair watch hees step, thees one. For Luis Gonzalez has hees heye on heem!"

There were too many eyes, feet, and hands in this remark for Fooey Mulligan to bother sorting them all out. And just then Nick Naldini came strolling up.

"Hot on the trail, are we, Hawkshaw?" inquired the lanky magician affably. Slightly put off at having his tête-à-tête with the good-looking blonde interrupted, the small detective shot Nick a glare.

"Who ees thees 'Awkshaw?" he hissed through a mouthful of gold fillings.

"Another private eye for your collection," grinned Nick. "Somewhat predating Sam Spade, though."

"Hi am not knoweeng thees 'Awkshaw,'" grumbled Luis Gonzalez coldly. "Meestair Bogart ees nevair playing heem in hees peectures."

With a sniff, the little man ambled off, teetering on his elevator heels, leaving Nick and Fooey to their own devices.

For a little while Luiz Gonzalez interrogated the villagers, but learned little that was useful to his investigations. They told him all about the fire-devil and how the mythical island hero Wakuaha had imprisoned the monster ages ago beneath the fiery mountain. None of this contributed to his concept of detective-work; and Luis Gonzalez was the proud possessor of a high school diploma, earned from a correspondence school on the mainland, and thus was too well-educated to give any credence to the local superstitions.

He wandered back to the trading-post, where Señor

Valdez was overseeing the repairs to his fire-blackened building. The gentlemanly old hidalgo could give the dwarfish detective little more information than he already possessed, although he patiently answered each question to the best of his ability.

Luiz Gonzalez knew all about the store-owner. He had looked him up in the police files before leaving Mantilla. The law enforcement officials there maintained rather complete dossiers on the more important citizens of the Luzon Union, and Felipe Mendoza Valdez was an important citizen by their standards. His family had made its home in these islands from the time of the first Spanish explorers. And he was, by all accounts, a highly respectable and law-abiding citizen.

The only one of the recent visitors to the island whom he had not yet found an opportunity to interrogate was the young Yankee geologist, John James Jones, whom he understood to be very ill. The young man was currently convalescing in one of the huts of the village, being tended by Señor Valdez' housekeeper. Every time Luis Gonzalez had poked his head in, the emaciated young American had been asleep under sedation applied by Prince Zarkon.

Thinking of Zarkon, the island Hawkshaw decided to look him up and see what the Man of Mysteries was doing. Luis Gonzalez had a healthy respect for the famous adventurer. He had looked him up in the police records before leaving Mantilla, too, and the dossier on the former Prince of Novenia was thick with information. Zarkon came with the highest of personal recommendations from the foremost law enforcement agencies in the world, including the FBI in Washington, the metropolitan police in London, Scotland Yard, the French Surete, Interpol itself, and such private crime-fighting bureaus as Doctor Palfrey's Z5 organization, which was affiliated with the United Nations. The credentials of Zarkon were most impressive indeed.

The Hispanic detective decided to check into what Zarkon was doing. It was not at all impossible that the Ultimate Man had some clues into the mysteries of the island which he had not as yet shared with Luis Gonzalez.

The little detective spotted Zarkon just as the man in gunmetal gray was leaving the village.

Something about the elusive, unobtrusive manner in which the Lord of the Unknown glided into the jungle caught the wary and alert eye of the small man.

It was obvious that Zarkon was trying to elude notice. His actions were not exactly furtive, but something about his manner roused the suspicions of Luiz Gonzalez. There was no questioning the fact that Zarkon did not wish to be seen. Whatever the nature of the mission on which the Man from Tomorrow was bound, it was, to one degree or another, clandestine.

So the dwarfish detective decided to follow the Omega Man and find out where he was going, and why. Quite obviously, if Zarkon was on the track of the murderer, it was to the intense personal interest of Señor Luis Gonzalez to know about it. And besides, there was another reason for his curiosity: it would be interesting, from a professional viewpoint, to see how the famous adventurer went about one of his own celebrated investigations.

So, moving with exaggerated caution, slipping from house to house, scuttling on teetering heels across the plowed fields, and then creeping from bush to bush along the outskirts of the jungle, the Luzon detective set about following Zarkon.

His attempts at self-concealment were ludicrous and

clumsy, but as Zarkon did not once look behind him as he entered the jungles and vanished from view, presumably the detective's attempts were successful.

Except from the rear.

For Scorchy Muldoon, bored by watching the islanders working on the repairs to the burnt-out trading-post, began restlessly looking around for something to do. His sharp eyes noticed Zarkon as the golden man in gunmetal gray slipped unobtrusively into the jungle, which swallowed him up. Always ready for action, Scorchy was about to follow his chief, hoping to join up with him in the jungle, when he saw the comical little Luzonian cop dogging Zarkon's heels.

Scorchy frowned, considering. The ridiculous little detective was obviously trying to follow Zarkon without himself being caught at it. Scorchy had no way of guessing his motives, but, after all, it did look suspicious. What did they really know about Señor Gonzalez, anyway? He had come to the island that morning in a motor-launch from Mantilla, and his police credentials seemed authentic enough, but there might be more to the clownish little detective than met the eye. And credentials can be borrowed, stolen, or faked.

Scorchy plunged into the jungle, following the scuttling little figure of the detective. Even in the thick brush and heavy gloom of the interior it was not hard to keep Señor Gonzalez in sight. His loud checked suit, flamboyant purple shirt, and silk tie of shrieking orange made him stand out even in the jungle.

Zarkon circled the base of the mountain, keeping deep within the depths of the jungle, and Señor Gonzalez clung to his trail, with Scorchy following *him.*

No one else saw them leave the village area.

CHAPTER 15

Zarkon Vanishes!

This was the second time in as many days that Scorchy Muldoon had gone cromping through the jungle, and he liked it even less the second time than he had the first.

Leaf-muck squelched juicily underfoot. Mud besplattered his shoes, socks, and trouser-legs. Vines kept making grabs at his neck like so many strangling nooses aimed at him by invisible Dacoits. Thorny, saw-edged leaves and bushes scratched his hands and plucked and tore at his jacket.

The little Irishman, whose temper was hair-trigger sensitive even at the best of times, cursed under his breath. The air was hot and muggy and thick with the stench of rotting leaves. It was hot and soon got hotter, until Scorchy began to sweat. This drew flies: and the flies of Rangatoa were nothing like their stateside cousins.

Back home, the buzzing mites were merely bothersome. Here in the Pacific, it seemed, they grew as big as hornets, bit like scorpions, and had a nasty habit of flying directly into your eyes.

No, it would not be an exaggeration to say that Scorchy was unfond of jungles. In fact, it would be the understatement of the year.

But the pugnacious little prizefighter clung doggedly to

the trail of Luis Gonzalez. The pop-eyed island Sherlock in the racetrack tout's zoot-suit was blundering and sloshing along, hitting as many mud-puddles as was Scorchy, if not a few more. And, erelong, there floated back to where Scorchy followed in the rear a sizzling stream of sotto-voce cussing, regrettably, in Spanish.

This was music to the ears of the feisty little Irishman. The wise men of yore never hit the nail on the head more accurately than when they voiced that age-old morsel of wisdom, that misery loves company.

If Scorchy had to crawl through the fly-buzzing jungle muck, sweating like a pig and mud-besplattered to the hips, it helped a little to know that the goggle-eyed Hispanic Hawkshaw was enjoying the experience no more than he was.

Where the jungle dwindled out and the swamps began, Scorchy paused, and ducked behind a conveniently-located tree, around which he peered irritatedly.

He did this because the man he was following had like-wise halted in his progress, and was now squatting be-hind a bush, on his hunkers, pop-eyes squinting through the leaves at something interesting up ahead.

From where he was hiding, Scorchy could not see Zarkon's whereabouts. But, since it was Zarkon whom Señor Luis Gonzalez had been shadowing all this time, it was an easy deduction to make that it was the Prince the detective was observing from his place of concealment.

Scorchy crept on tiptoes to a better vantage-point behind a stand of rattling bamboo. From here he could survey the scene much better without himself being visi-ble.

Señor Gonzalez was crouching painfully about a dozen yards away; the little man seemed to be squeezing himself into the smallest possible area, probably because the bush behind which he had chosen to hide was really too small for this purpose.

Scorchy grinned wickedly. It did his heart good to observe the sorry conditions of Señor Gonzalez' raiment, considering the dilapidated appearance of his own clothes. The dwarfed detective's racetrack finery had suffered more than a little from his trip through the damp, muddy undergrowth. And, for that matter, his snap-brimmed fedora would never be the same again, not after having been dislodged from atop his head by a low-hanging vine which had precipitated the item of headwear into the gooey depths of a large puddle. But, undeterred, the Hispanic Hawkshaw had tracked his quarry to its goal.

Zarkon himself was behaving in a rather curious manner, Scorchy noticed.

Approaching the hut in which John James Jones had been living until his ordeal in the swamp had necessitated his hospitalization, the Ultimate Man paid no attention to the building itself, but examined the lobster-pots.

Several of these wire traps, designed to catch unwary crustaceans of an edible variety, were suspended by cords from the pilings upon which Johnny Jones's hut was built out over the deep waters of the swamp. It was hardly likely that the young geologist had actually caught lobsters in these contrivances, since the creatures thrive only in saltwater and would tend to avoid the stagnant waters of the swamp, but obviously some comparable varieties of the genus *Crustacea* inhabited the boggy depths, whereby the Yank had varied his diet from time to time.

"Now, whaddaya s'pose the chief's checkin' out them dang pots for?" murmured Scorchy to himself.

Apparently satisfying himself as to the harmlessness of the suspended traps, Zarkon next circled the foundations of the hut and ascended the slope of the mountain's base to the ledge on which Scorchy had been attacked by the ogre. Closely scanning the ground, Zarkon began to ascend the trail, which wound up the side of the volcano, zigzagging back and forth to the top.

Suddenly Señor Gonzalez jumped to his feet and raced out of the jungle to the edge of the swamp.

Craning his head about, his grotesque pop-eyes staring up towards the top of the mountain, the little detective seemed very excited about something.

Scorchy's curiosity began to get the better of him.

He came out of cover and trotted up behind the little Hawkshaw.

"Here, now, what're you after followin' the chief for, anyway?" he growled from directly behind the detective.

The little man squawked, jumped two inches in the air, and came down goggling over his shoulder at Scorchy.

He gulped, mopped his face with a purple silk handkerchief, looking relieved.

"Ees eet hyou, Señor Scorchy," he gasped. "*Hai, caramba*, but Hi thought eet was the *monstair!*"

"I'll 'monster' you, Funny-Lookin'," bristled the Irishman. "How come you're tailin' the chief?"

Stuttering excitedly, the detective flapped his hands about, calling Scorchy's attention to the mountain trail.

Scorchy looked, blinked, rubbed his eyes, and looked again.

Although it would have taken the most agile and acrobatic of men several minutes more to reach the peak of Mount Rangatoa, *Zarkon was no longer anywhere on the trail.*

"Huh! I don't get it," grunted Scorchy unbelievingly.

Fairly bobbing up and down in his excitement, the little detective waggled his head in violent agreement.

"While Hi was watcheeng, eet happans!" he burbled in a very ecstasy of agitation.

"*What* happened?" demanded Scorchy in rising alarm. "Make some sense, willya?"

"The *Preence!* He ees *vanisheeng!* Right before of my heyes!" yammered Señor Gonzalez.

"Oh, yeah?" demanded Scorchy excitedly. He grabbed the little Sherlock by one arm. "C'mon, then, Louie. Let's get up there and have us a look-see. Somethin' funny's goin' on around here. You packin' a rod?"

Nodding wildly, Señor Gonzalez plucked from the waistband of his trousers a perfectly enormous blue-steel revolver. This miniature cannon looked big enough to knock down elephants.

"Good enough," Scorchy grunted. "Climb, Louie! I got me a hunch this here case is about to break wide open!"

They clambered up the slope and began scrambling along the ascending trail which Zarkon had followed.

But it looked as if the Lord of the Unknown had literally vanished into thin air right before their eyes. For not the slightest clue could they find as to where he had gone!

CHAPTER 16

Where Angels Fear to Tread

For a while that morning, Phoenicia Mulligan hung around the native village. She chatted with some of the island women, who knew Spanish well enough, although at unpredictable intervals they would inject a word or phrase in their own lingo, which the attractive blonde did not speak.

She watched the naked brown children scuttle up palms to dislodge coconuts into nets held stretched out beneath; she amused herself by helping them haul in their fishing nets from the end of one of the long promontories which encircled the lagoon like two outstretched and curving arms. She helped them hoe yams and pick bananas. Eventually, she became a trifle bored.

And when Fooey Mulligan became bored she also became restless. At such times, she generally tended to alleviate the tedium of the moment by getting into trouble.

The blond heiress had managed in one way or another to get into—and, luckily, out of—an awful lot of trouble in her time. She still remembered being treed by a pride of hungry lions when on safari in the grasslands of Kenya, because she had obstinately insisted on taking a morning stroll, against all objections by the safari leader that to stray from camp alone could be dangerous.

He had been right, of course. But then, danger *per se* had never bothered Fooey Mulligan. In fact, she rather liked getting into trouble.

It was usually more fun getting into trouble than it was getting out of it, she had found. But the alluring aura of peril that clung about the getting-into part she always found breathlessly exciting. If the getting-out-of portion of the experience was usually scary, often heart-stoppingly so, well: that was the price you had to pay for the thrill of the thing, that was all.

Life in the island village of Tarapaho was happy, tranquil, and dreadfully repetitious, she soon discovered, after a dull but pleasurable morning of strolling about.

Fooey decided to get into some trouble, if only to break the monotony. At times like this she hungered for a little action. A bit of hell-raising never hurt, she thought confidently to herself. And where better to flirt with peril than up on the haunted mountain itself, near the smoking crater where the ogre seemed to lurk?

The fire that had destroyed Zarkon's gear had also ruined her expectations for a deliciously exciting morning. For Phoenicia had firmly intended joining in on the expedition down into the lava-filled crater.

Now that the trip was off, it occurred to the blond girl that it would be fun trying it on her own. She had gone spelunking many a time, exploring dark and dangerous caves—and how much worse could a descent into the smoking crater of an active volcano be, after all? Outside of the blistering heat, the suffocating fumes, the risk of falling into a lake of molten lava, it ought to be as much fun as venturing into a subterranean cavern.

And the possibility of catching a glimpse of the weird marauding monster on the prowl, well, that only added a little spice to the fare.

Now, Phoenicia Mulligan was no fool. Although she had a headstrong tendency to go galloping into places where any self-respecting angel might fear to tread, she also did it with the decided intention of coming out again more-or-less unscathed.

Hence, when getting into tight spots, Fooey was sensible enough to take a few reasonable precautions.

For a little poking around inside the crater of Mount Rangatoa, Fooey Mulligan decided she needed an assist from an able-bodied type. So she went looking for one of the Omega men, fully confident of her ability to coax, tease, shame, or bully one of them into accompanying her on the adventure.

She was rather hoping to find Ace Harrigan, for the frank, guileless, and good-looking young aviator had made a decided impression on her. Without wasting time considering it, she knew better than to try to persuade Prince Zarkon into the scheme. The Man of Mysteries, she knew, would be too staid, too sober, too sensible, to encourage her in such an extravagance. She didn't for a moment doubt that Zarkon would dope her, tie her up, or hypnotize her, or something, to keep her out of trouble.

Not finding Ace anywhere about, the blond girl went hunting for Scorchy. The fiery-thatched bantamweight had a disrespect for caution, an eye for trouble, and a thirst for danger equal to her own, she knew. If ever there was a perfect henchman for her shenanigans, it was Aloysius Murphy Muldoon, he of the flying fists, the runaway temper, and the susceptibility where curvaceous blondes were concerned.

Of course, at about this same time, Scorchy Muldoon was well on his way to getting into trouble all by himself. The feisty little boxer was at that very moment sneaking through the jungle, hot on the tracks of Chicago Louie

Gonzalez, whose suspicious actions had roused his curiosity. But Phoenicia, of course, could not have known anything of this.

What she eventually found, as things turned out, was Nick Naldini.

The long-legged vaudevillian with the Mephisto beard was lazily stretched out under a palm tree, surrounded by a giggling bevy of brown-skinned young beauties whom he was amusing by some minor tricks of stage magic. He plucked flowers from the girls' ears, coins from their hair, lighted cigarettes from their noses, juggled these, made them multiply, made them vanish, made them reappear, and so on. The girls were loving it, and Nick began to feel that he was getting to first base, at least, with more than a few of the dark-eyed, sarong-clad charmers.

Hence, when Miss Phoenicia Mulligan popped into view, imperiously summoning his aid, the former magician was not exactly thrilled to pieces. The island girls were snuggling near, the weather was balmy, and Nick felt lazy. He was, in fact, disinclined to lend comfort and assistance to a mission he knew his chief would disapprove of.

But Phoenicia Mulligan had not reached the ripe age of twenty-whatever-it-was without having long since mastered the fine feminine arts of making men do what she wanted them to do. As any number of Park Avenue playboys, Southampton sportsmen, and members of the horsey set in San Francisco, Honolulu, and Palm Beach could have attested, once Fooey Mulligan set her mind to go on an outing, all males in the immediate vicinity are automatically helpless to resist her blandishments.

Thus, rather dazedly, Nick Naldini found himself some ten minutes later clambering gingerly up the slopes of the volcano, lending a hand to a pretty blonde in white slacks named Phoenicia. With only the haziest notion of what he was doing there, or why, or how he had been bamboozled into backing her up on this crazy jaunt.

They reached the peak of the mountain and paused for a breather. Nick, a trifle winded, sagged into a sitting position on a conveniently-placed boulder and began swabbing his brow while confusedly striving to remember what variety of female sorcery the determined heiress had worked upon him to get him out of that cozy cluster of island cuties and into this nutty, hare-brained venture.

Whatever the nature of her wiles, he thought to himself, they were efficient. Fooey Mulligan's talents at wheedling men and at getting her way with them worked like magic. Heaven help the masculine half of the voting citizenry, thought Nick to himself, if the blond girl ever decided to go into politics. With her abilities to boondoggle anything in long pants, she'd be redecorating the White House in no time!

"C'mon, lazy-bones," the girl chided. "Only a little further to the top."

"*Whoof,*" he commented. "Only a little further to the oxygen-tent, you mean! Give a fellow a break, can't you? This dang mountain'll still be here ten minutes from now."

"Can't take it, eh?" She grinned. "Gonna let a mere slip of a girl beat ya to the top?"

"Mere slip, nothing," he groaned with a theatrical grimace. "You got enough get-up-and-go for both of us, Fooey, you phoney! Me, I'm sittin' right here till my breath catches up with me. You wanta break the local speed records, go ahead . . ."

Phoenicia made a little face, stuck out her tongue at him saucily, and flounced off to finish the climb. Nick stubbornly sat where he was, confident that the devil-may-care girl couldn't get into trouble for a couple minutes, at least. When it came to mountain-climbing, the girl had the agility of the proverbial mountain-goat.

Phoenicia was too restless to stick around, waiting for Nick to get over being winded. The girl found the fresh air, sparkling sunlight, and excitement of the climb exhilarating. She tackled the remainder of the slope with zest, energetically clambering from rock to rock, determined to scale the topmost peak and be seated there, lazily admiring the view, by the time the long-legged vaudevillian came groaning, grumbling, and grouching up to the top himself.

Things turned out otherwise, however. As things usually did whenever Miss Fooey Mulligan decided to go off in search of an adventure all by her lonesome.

Here at the peak of the volcanic mountain, white vapor blew blindingly, tossed about by the winds that whistled strongly about the height.

A dense plume of white steam, smelling strongly of sulphur and blistering-hot lava, seethed up from the mouth of the crater. It streamed from the wide-lipped bowl of rock and was whipped about and torn to flying tatters in the gusting sea breeze.

Suddenly a huge, lumbering shape loomed black and monstrous through the flying mists. It was so unexpected, somehow, and it happened so fast, that Phoenicia was taken by surprise. The monstrous silhouette seemed to materialize out of thin air, like an apparition conjured into existence in a single eye-blink by the wand of a magician.

The volcano ogre was on the prowl—

And Phoenicia Mulligan was directly in its path!

CHAPTER 17

The Hidden Cave

The blond girl froze, her heart pounding like a triphammer. She was suffocated by the suddenness with which the monstrous apparition had appeared. And for a moment she could hardly catch a breath, so stifling was the thundering of her pulse.

A split-second later, the girl recovered her poise and also her pluck. The monster had not seen her yet. That was obvious, because otherwise the thing would probably have come at her, steaming paws outreaching, to burn and maim and kill.

Fooey Mulligan blinked, a grin forming mischievously. The blond adventuress could hardly believe her luck—now that she realized the monster had not glimpsed her and was not going to attack.

She hadn't really expected to stumble on the monster. All she had in mind was a little hell-raising to relieve the tedium of a rather dull and boring morning when nothing much seemed to be going on in Rangatoa. But here she was, actually within eyeshot of the murder monster!

The girl excitedly complimented herself on her extraordinary luck. When she had decided to climb the mountain and poke around the top of it, hunting for clues, she hadn't really thought it likely she would catch another glimpse of the famous fire-devil. The elusive and mysterious troll seemed to pop up at the most unexpected of times. But, by golly, luck or no luck, she had done her mountain-climbing at just the right time to catch the weird creature lumbering about its uncanny business. There was no doubt about it—there it was, all right!

The girl ducked down behind the rock on which she had been sitting, just in case the burning ogre should turn around and happen to notice her. Lips parted, breathless with excitement, April-colored eyes glistening with the pure thrill of it, she peered over the rock to see what the ogre was doing now.

The huge creature seemed to be lifting one ponderous leg over the lip of the crater, as if intending to jump into the lava-lake below!

In the next instant, flying white fog blotted out the scene. Fooey bit her lip and cussed to herself with a *most* unladylike oath.

The next moment, however, the whipping wind tore a hole through the mist and she could see that the ogre was climbing over the edge of the crater and seemed to be feeling around for a foothold on the inner wall.

Then the huge shape ducked below the lip of the crater and vanished.

This, obviously, was her golden opportunity!

If she was lucky, thought Phoenicia to herself, she might be able to see where it was that the volcano monster hid itself when it vanished mysteriously, as it had so often done after one of its marauding expeditions.

Her blue eyes sparkled with excitement. If she could find a clue to the secret of the ogre's hiding-place—or, better yet, if she could actually discover the whereabouts of its hidden lair—*wow!*

Not only would she have stolen a big march on Prince

Zarkon—but she would have a darn good chance to crack the mystery wide open, all by herself!

The chance was too mouth-wateringly tempting to pass up. She couldn't just crouch here and let this priceless opportunity slip through her fingers.

Of course, the commonsensical thing to do would be to wait until Nick Naldini caught up to her. Then the two of them could follow the brute; after all, the stage magician probably packed a gun.

But Fooey Mulligan simply would not have been Fooey Mulligan if she had chosen the safer course of action, or had done the thing that common sense recommended. And besides (thought she to herself), why should she give Nick Naldini a share in the credit for busting the mystery? This was her discovery, and hers alone.

Cautiously she peeped out of her hiding-place again. The monster had obviously descended into the crater by now. Since it was below the crater's lip, there was no longer any danger that the creature might chance to look around and spot her watching its movements. Now was her chance!

Phoenicia left her place of concealment behind the big boulder and darted up the few yards of slope which led to the edge of the crater.

At the lip of the bowl-like depression she paused and carefully looked over the edge, careful lest the monster see her from below. It was hard to see anything at first, her eyes watering at the sting of the hot, sulphur-smelling steam. Blinking to clear her vision, for a moment she could see nothing but tear-blur and flying vapor. Then a sudden gust of wind parted the vapor like a curtain, and she got a clear look down at the inside of the crater-wall.

The monster was descending by a zigzag ledge a foot or so wide. Due to the perspective, and the blowing vapor, and the ruddy light beating up from the crater floor, this narrow ledge would have been virtually impossible to see and would have gone unnoticed, had it not been for the dark, thick shape of the huge creature inching its way along it.

Suddenly the volcano ogre ducked underneath an overhanging rock, and did not emerge again into view.

"By golly, there must be a crevice down there—a cave or something," the girl muttered to herself excitedly. "You can't see the opening because that rock hides it from view up above. Wow!"

The transcendent importance of her discovery went to the blond girl's head. The smart thing to do, the judicious thing, the sensible thing, would be to go back down the mountain, find Zarkon, and announce that she had found the ogre's den.

At the very least, she should have waited for Nick Naldini to catch up with her.

But Phoenicia would not have been Phoenicia had she been quite that methodical, calm, or level-headed. Adventure beckoned just beyond the crater's rim; mystery sang its siren-song in her ear. And Fooey Mulligan, being Fooey Mulligan, succumbed to its irresistible allure.

Without a thought as to the possible consequences, the girl swung one leg over the rim of the crater—felt around for a foothold—found the beginning of the all-but-invisible ledge that went zigzagging down to the hidden mouth of the cave—swung over the edge and vanished in the flying clouds of steam.

When Nick came puffing and groaning to the top a split-second later, she was nowhere to be seen.

Phoenicia Mulligan had simply vanished from the face of the earth.

Nick groaned and rolled his eyes heavenwards.

"Dang that nutty blonde," he cursed feebly. "If I don't find her, the chief'll have my hide!"

CHAPTER 18

A Secret Passage

The dwarfish detective, with Scorchy Muldoon at his heels, went scrambling up the rocky trail on which Prince Zarkon had so mysteriously vanished into thin air.

The volcanic mountain, obviously very old, was of a remarkably low elevation. Quite likely, Mount Rangatoa had blown its top, so too speak, many times during the aeons of its history; each time, this had crumbled away the cone of the volcano in its tapering upper parts. What was left by this time was a mere stump of what had once, geological ages ago, probably been a soaring, Fujiyama-type mountain. And erosion had done the rest of the job, crumbling the hardened lava-streams into rich, loamy soil, building up a land-mass around the tall cone-shaped peak. This had doubtless been the genesis of Rangatoa Island, itself.

By the zigzag ledge, therefore, it was only a short trip up to the top of the mountain. An agile man with sound wind could accomplish the climb—here on this side of the mountain, anyway—in mere minutes.

But Zarkon could not possibly have gotten to the top of the volcano during the very brief time that his actions were hidden from the watching eyes of Señor Luis Gonzalez.

Scorchy reasoned this out for himself, and said as much to the little Hispanic detective, who stood there on the trail, gnawing his straggly mustache in a fury of bafflement.

"The chief musta either gone off the trail somewhere, or . . ." he mumbled, letting his words ebb into silence. *Or what?* Scorchy couldn't think of an *or what* to add to the above remark.

"Eet ees that 'or hwhat' that bothairs me," said the pop-eyed little man. "Hwhere could 'ee have gone, eef 'ee went off the trail, thees Preence? See for hyourself, Señor Scorchy, the mountain, she ees smooth an' unbroken to eithair side."

Chewing on his calloused knuckles, Scorchy had to agree. He knew Zarkon well enough to know that the Ultimate Man was unpredictable and full of surprises. Very often, the Prince was several jumps ahead of everyone else connected with a case, and had things doped out in his head. Since Zarkon usually kept his thoughts to himself on such occasions, he more often than not would pull some uncanny trick, like this one, catching everybody else by surprise. But popping out of existence, while clinging to the sheer cliff-like side of a mountain by broad daylight, with two men looking on, well—*this* trick was a bit uncannier than most of the ones he'd pulled within Scorchy's memory.

For want of any more-reasonable explanation of Zarkon's disappearance, Scorchy in despair turned to the standard ingredients of melodrama.

"All right," he grumped, "so maybe there's a hidden door here, maskin' a secret passage, or something!"

By way of emphasis, Scorchy slapped the sheer wall of rock right where he was standing.

And in the next instant he uttered a shrill yelp and jumped nearly a foot into the air—

For the rock he had touched just then—slid inwards!

A black rectangular cavity was thus revealed. A yawning entrance whose black mouth gave upon a tunnel hollowed into the solid rock of the mountain!

"H-holy J-Jumpin' Shamrocks!" gulped the little prizefighter, his eyes bulging with astonishment. "Open, Sesame! And lookee here, Hawkshaw, we got us a secret cave!"

Señor Luis Gonzalez was visibly impressed. He had heard a lot about the fantastic exploits of the Omega men, for their deeds were legendary among the cops of every nation. But the yarns he had listened to he had always privately considered pure guff, sheer fable, tall tales told to flummox dopes. Now, however, he saw the tangible evidence that this famous band of crime-fighters were in reality the miracle-workers legend made them out to be.

"*Hai, caramba!*" the dwarfish detective breathed, swarthy features paling to the hue of sour milk. "S-Señor Scorchy, 'ow deed hyou do eet?"

The Pride of the Muldoons had the rare presence of mind to shrug nonchalantly, feigning a casual boredom he did not in the slightest really feel.

"Oh, shucks, Louie," he said carelessly, buffing the nails of one hand on his lapel, then holding up that hand to admire the digits. "Nuttin' to it, really! Me and the boys, why, we gotta lotta tricks up our sleeve; *you* know how it is!"

He tried to pretend that opening trick doors to secret caves in the sides of volcanoes was the sort of thing he did every day in the week. If his offhand manner actually gulled Luis Gonzalez into swallowing this, it was only because the crook-chaser from Luzon was still bedazedly marveling over the feat—which had actually been nothing but the most incredible stroke of pure luck, of course.

"Guess the chief found this here hidey-hole, too," yawned Scorchy with a pretense of boredom. "Well, while we're here, Louie, what say we take us a look-see down inside. Be kinda nice, huh, to be in on the wrap-up?"

"Whatevair hyou say, Señor Scorchy," hissed the little cop, gold teeth sparklingly revealed in a dazed smile. His pop-eyes followed Scorchy with a sheen in them that could only have been hero-worship as the bantamweight boxer poked his head gingerly into the opening his chance touch had revealed.

A moment later, Scorchy ducked into the black mouth of the hidden opening and vanished. Señor Luis Gonzalez squared his broadly-padded shoulders manfully, and tip-toed after the intrepid little Irishman.

From the expression on his ugly face, it was apparent that the redheaded little Irishman had dislodged "H*om*phrey Bogart" from his pedestal in the esteem of the comical little detective of the islands.

The tunnel in the side of the volcano turned out to be narrower than a miser's generosity, and blacker than a vampire's sins.

Some hand—from the chisel-marks in the stone, it could not have been Dame Nature's—had cut the secret tunnel deep into the solid stone of the volcano's flanks.

It had been, obviously, a crude and hasty job, with few luxuries. To get through it you had to walk sideways and inch along with your feet in a crablike shuffle.

Scorchy had his gun out, ready for action, as he took

the lead. There was just no telling where this long black hole led to, but if this was the way the chief had gone, Scorchy was determined to follow it to the end. And there could hardly be any question that Zarkon had ducked in here when he had, presumably, melted into thin air. Probably, the Man of Mysteries had carried one of his radio gadgets with him, reasoned Scorchy: probably the midget gizmo that could detect metal even through solid rock. This made sense, because the "door" to the hidden tunnel had turned out to be painted plaster molded on a steel frame: Scorchy had noticed this when he had stepped through the entrance into the black tunnel.

"*Heest!* Señor Scorchy," the dwarfish detective hissed in his ear a moment later.

"Yeah? What is it, Louie?"

"Light up ahead. Ees eet that hwe are come to the lair of the monstair?" whispered the Luzonian.

Scorchy craned his neck about, peering up the tunnel. There was indeed a weird bluish glimmer faintly visible where it gleamed along the edges of the chisel-scrapes in the soft rock.

"Sure, an' Oi'm after guessin' that yer right, me bucko," breathed Scorchy, lapsing into his stage Irishman's brogue, as he usually did when the situation began to heat up and looked to be getting hotter in the next few moments. "Are yez packin' yer rod?"

The detective gave a golden-toothed grin, displaying the enormous revolver he had worn concealed under his coat.

"Then le's git goin'," burbled Scorchy, grinning excitedly. Things had been fairly dull up till now—a mere matter of two murders, a couple of disappearances, and a mysterious fire—but Scorchy had a hunch some *real* excitement lay dead ahead.

The runty Irishman had his own weapon with him, of course. But it was one of the special gimmicks Prince Zarkon insisted that his lieutenants use: fired by compressed air, the trick revolvers shot bullets made of hard rubber. These were remarkably effective when used against human foes, because the Omega men were trained experts in knowing where to hit their enemies with the rubber bullets in order to incapacitate them harmlessly. The major nerve centers—exposed clumps of sensitive ganglia, like the "funny bone" part of elbow or kneecap, the solar plexus, and so on—these were their usual targets.

But where the dickens were the sensitive places on a volcano devil? Scorchy swore under his breath, glad that Señor Luis Gonzalez packed a real rod that spit steel-jacketed lead. This spare-the-poor-crook's-life side of his chief's character was one part of Zarkon's personality with which Scorchy Muldoon quarreled.

To his way of thinking, the best sort of criminal is the one with a couple of slugs pumped into him. And the runty redhead had a hunch that guns would be out and blamming away before much longer.

Just how accurate this hunch was, Scorchy couldn't have guessed until he and Chicago Louie turned the next corner and found themselves the spectators gazing upon an astounding tableau!

CHAPTER 19

In the Ogre's Den

Phoenicia found descending into the crater of a live volcano a bit more exciting than she had calculated.

The blond adventuress found danger mighty stimulating. But this latest madcap scheme of hers provided just a bit more of a stimulus than she had really bargained for.

For one thing, it was almost impossible to breathe. Live steam and stinking fumes of hot sulphur came billowing up from the bubbling lava-lake below. Her eyes watered uncontrollably, blurring her vision, and her mouth and the lining of her throat ached painfully from the choking vapors.

The ledge itself was narrow and precipitous and scary. Bits of crumbling rock rolled loosely underfoot. At times the rocky footpath shrank until it was only inches wide; and even at its widest it was pretty difficult to negotiate. If she had a block and tackle, a safety line, or regular mountain-scaling equipment, it wouldn't have been so tough. But, of course, she had none of these things.

Where the ledge narrowed until it was only inches wide, the girl was forced to hug the inner crater wall, inching along on her tiptoes, with the heels of her shoes hanging out over empty space.

The rocky wall to which she clung, at such times, was blisteringly hot. She hung on gamely, grimly feeling her way down the steep incline of the ledge with a cautious toe, trying to ignore the pain in her fingers and also trying not to think about that bubbling lake of cherry-red, glowing lava which seethed and slurped and slopped beneath her heels.

One false step, she knew, would precipitate her into that pool of liquid rock. She would be fried like a flounder on a hot griddle within half a second. This was not the most cheerful thing to contemplate, and at times the plucky girl gulped, trying to keep down her breakfast.

Luckily, Fooey Mulligan had been in plenty of tight spots before, and could keep a cool head and steady nerves even in situations as scary as this present one. Over the years she had gotten herself into a lot of tricky circumstances like this one. Always before, she had managed to get out of them pretty much in one piece. So the girl had confidence in her ability to come through the squeeze with a whole skin.

It was fortunate for Phoenicia Mulligan, however, that this particular volcano had a particularly shallow crater. Almost before she knew it, the danger-loving heiress found herself at the entrance to the hole in the wall into which the ogre must have ducked.

Fooey hung on to the stony outcropping which overhung the mouth of the cave and prevented it from being seen from above, pondering her next step.

She really hadn't stopped to think what she intended to do at this juncture. The blond girl had a tendency to just plunge headlong into a dangerous situation, without thinking out her moves in advance. She trusted her proven abilities to keep her head clear, her hands steady, and her nerves unshaken during any sort of an emergency.

Up till now, these abilities had pulled her through. But Phoenicia had never quite gotten herself into a scrape as tight and tough as this one, and now the girl gritted her teeth and cussed a little, wishing she had thought about what to do once she actually got down here.

It seemed, even to her, incredibly foolhardy to go climbing into the ogre's den, knowing good and well that the man-killing monster was in there somewhere, prowling around. It was on a par with walking into a grizzly's cave, aware that the grizzly was currently in residence.

But—what else was there to do? She didn't like the idea of going back without really having accomplished much of anything. She could imagine how Nick would snicker at the knowledge that she had climbed all the way down into the crater to the very monster's very front door, then lost her nerve at the last moment, and had to come shame-facedly back. Retreat from a trouble-spot was not in Fooey's character!

On the other hand, it was virtually suicidal to go climbing into the ogre's lair, with the creature in there somewhere.

Sure, she had her gun with her, but so what? She had already emptied the pistol smack into the monster's chest at point-blank range, without even slowing it down. What she *really* needed, in the present instance, was a bazooka. Or a hand-grenade!

But she had neither.

And by now, Nick Naldini would surely have caught his breath and would have scaled the remainder of the slope. Reaching the peak, the lanky magician would at this very moment be scouting around, hunting for her. She could just picture the grin on his long-chinned, Mephisto-bearded face when he saw her climbing back out of the volcano, a trembling, gooey mass of the shivers!

The blond girl clenched her jaw stubbornly.

Anything was better than that, she decided. Well . . . almost anything, she amended.

So there was nothing to do but venture in and beard the ogre in his hidey-hole.

And, besides, she was getting tired of hanging on to this hunk of hot rock.

So, drawing a deep breath, ignoring the sting of sulphur-reek, the girl ducked her head down and squeezed herself into the black mouth of the cave.

Once inside, Phoenicia found that the air was cooler and much more breathable.

The cave seemed pitch-dark at first, despite a dim glow which seeped in through the cave-mouth from the lava-pit at the crater's floor. The cherry-red light did little to alleviate the dense blackness.

Then, in a moment, her eyes adjusted themselves to a faint pulse of luminance from somewhere up ahead. By the faint blue light glimmering up ahead at the end of the tunnel, and the dim red glow beating in through the entrance, she could just make out the broken rocky floor underfoot and something of the low-hanging roof.

She began to go forward, bumping her head a couple of times on the uneven roof.

It was slow going, but at the end of the tunnel the rocky walls widened out into a large chamber.

At the entrance to this inner chamber, Phoenicia Mulligan stopped short. Her eyes widened at the scene which she now saw before her.

The blue light came from a mercury-vapor lamp hung from a projection on the ceiling.

The floor of the cave was a deep pit, hollowed out in such a manner that it left a rocky ledge around the circular wall of this chamber, about three feet wide.

At the bottom of the pit in the chamber's floor, an irregular mass of mineral was exposed to view.

It was a rough, pitted mass of something resembling pure metal. But the metal itself was unrecognizable. A gray, slick stuff, shedding just the feeblest glow of yellowish-green light. She had never seen or heard of anything that looked like that, and could not imagine what it was.

Not that she had much time to think about it.

For there, crouching on the ledge which ran around the inside of the chamber, was the ogre in all its hideousness!

The monster was leaning over the pit which had been hollowed out in the floor of the chamber, obviously in order to expose the glowing mass of peculiar, unearthly metal.

At her appearance, the troll looked up.

It had no face. No face at all. Neither nose nor mouth nor ears. Two slits formed its eyes: the remainder of its visage was a smooth expanse of brownish substance which looked like solid rock. At least, the monster's head and face seemed to be coated with scaled, flaky, irregular coatings of something like rock.

It had a barrel torso, massive humped shoulders, thick gorilloid arms that were wider around than a grown man's upper thighs. These arms ended in mitten-like paws.

Spotting the girl in the entrance, frozen there in amazement, the monster got to its feet. It moved amazingly fast for anything as huge and as obviously heavy as it was.

It came lunging at her, huge paws out-thrust to catch and grab.

This time, the paws weren't smoking-hot. Nor did they dribble molten lava.

She could see that they were not really monster-paws at all, but thick, mitten-like protective gloves fashioned from some tough, durable, heat-resistant substance.

She could also see that the monster's head was a heavy helmet of some indefinable brown material. Its slitted eyes were actually recessed plates of inch-thick transparent glass or quartz. Because through them she could see the eyes of the person who wore the helmet, and the mittens, and the heavy protective suit.

And she screamed!

Not so much because the man in the monster-like suit was making a lunge for her. But because the eyes which peered through those thick transparent goggles were eyes that she recognized—

CHAPTER 20

Duel to the Death

What happened next was such a surprise to Phoenicia Mulligan that the blond girl actually forgot to be scared!

Because, even as she uttered a stifled shriek, another figure appeared in the blue-lit chamber. It seemed to materialize abruptly, as if by magic. It was only a moment later that Fooey saw from whence it had so swiftly sprung. For there was another cave-entrance on the far side of the chamber.

The figure which sprang out of the second tunnel was none other than that of Prince Zarkon. Phoenicia sagged limply against the side of the cave, gustily heaving a sigh of heart-felt relief. Never in all her days had she been as glad to see someone as she was to see the Ultimate Man at that moment.

Catching the expression in her eyes—sensing that another stranger had intruded into its hidden sanctum—the ogre turned slowly to see Zarkon emerge into sight.

The man in gunmetal gray poised for only an instant on the brink of the pit. Then he sprang across it to the farther side with an agility that would have done credit to the skills of a veteran acrobat.

The monster whirled about clumsily, paws reaching for Zarkon. But the Man of Mysteries was no longer there.

Ducking lithely beneath the groping paws of the volcano monster, the Prince darted to the wall of the cave. There leaned a variety of metal tools which Phoenicia Mulligan had not as yet had time to so much as notice.

Pickaxes, long-handled pincers, and pronged implements the girl did not recognize were there in a row, as well as power-drills and core-samplers and an ordinary shovel.

This last was the nearest to Zarkon. The Man from Tomorrow snatched it up and whirled it in the ogre's face, driving the monster back, step by stumbling step.

But two could play at this particular game, it seemed. For in its lurching, clumsy retreat the ogre came within reach of the tools, too; one of which it picked up in its thick paws.

Brandishing the heavy tool, the monster now came at Zarkon.

Phoenicia's heart was in her throat as she saw that the murder monster had now armed itself with a pickax!

It swung the ax at Zarkon. Again he glided aside, as agile and elusive as a wisp of smoke.

But Phoenicia uttered a frightened gasp, and put her knuckles to her mouth and bit them. For if but one of those savage, swinging blows ever connected, the ax which the ogre was wielding could crush Zarkon's skull like an eggshell under a hammer.

Zarkon retreated, step by step, until he could go no farther.

Then, lifting his shovel in a two-handed grip across his chest, he began using it to protect himself with, employing the metal tool like a quarterstaff.

Blow after blow of the great ax he caught, fended off, glanced aside. But still the monster pressed forward, driving Zarkon back inch by inch, swinging the heavy pickax in merciless swipes.

Within mere moments the ogre had Zarkon cornered against the entrance to the tunnel which led back the way Phoenicia had come—into the crater.

To retreat into the hole, the Ultimate Man would have had to relinquish his only defense, for the shovel was too long to fit into the entrance.

Phoenicia crouched against the wall, her heart pounding, helpless to intervene in this grim duel to the death.

This was the astonishing tableau upon which Scorchy Muldoon and Señor Luis Gonzalez stumbled half-a-second later. They emerged from the second tunnel only a few moments after Zarkon did. The Man from Tomorrow, obviously, had been only moments before them. Obviously, the Prince had concealed himself just within the entrance to the second tunnel and had been standing there for some time, observing the actions of the volcano ogre without letting himself be seen.

It had been the danger to Phoenicia Mulligan which had drawn Prince Zarkon out of hiding. Seeing the monster charging at the girl, the man in gunmetal gray had sprung to her defense. And now Zarkon himself was in danger. He could retreat no farther from the savage swings of the deadly pickax, and he could not enter the tunnel without putting down his only means of defense, thus exposing himself to the death-dealing ax.

So he did the one thing possible—

He stepped forward, directly into the monster's path! Blocking the pickax with the shovel-handle, Zarkon reversed his grip on the tool suddenly, and gave the monster a ringing clout alongside the head with the edge of the shovel-blade.

The ringing blow would have cracked a grizzly's skull or brained a gorilla. However, it hardly even dazed the man in the monster-suit; he lurched back only a single step, shaking his head dizzily, as if to clear his wits, then came forward again.

But that single step backwards was all that Prince Zarkon needed to put into action the plan his swift wits had conjured up.

He sprang to the brink of the ledge—teetered there for the tiniest fraction of a second—and in the next instant, he had launched himself into space!

Phoenicia Mulligan shrieked!

The pit was at its widest here. The girl could see that Prince Zarkon could not possibly leap across to the ledge on the farther side of the chamber. He could only fall into the pit where that mysterious mass of gray metal glowed with its eerie, uncanny, greenish-yellow radiance. And somehow she guessed that that gruesome radiation was—*deadly*.

But Zarkon neither fell into the pit of glowing metal nor attempted to reach the farther side of the ledge which circled the walls of the round chamber.

Instead, he had sprung up into the air. Legs bent into a crouch, his muscles like coiled steel springs, launched the Man of Marvels up into the air.

His upstretched hands brushed against the metal-shielded wire by which current was fed into the mercury-vapor lamp which hung suspended from a rocky projection of the roof.

Brushed—slipped—and *clung!*

Now Zarkon dangled by his fingertips alone, swinging above the pit of glowing metal.

Recovering from the blow of the shovel, which had only momentarily stunned it, the ogre lumbered to the brink of the ledge and swung back the pickax for a blow that would slay or cripple Zarkon.

But that blow never landed.

Instead, two unexpected things happened almost within the same instant.

Nick Naldini, looking somewhat disheveled and considerably singed, stuck his head into the chamber from the crater tunnel, took in the situation at one astounded glance, and fired his air-pistol at the ogre.

He instinctively did not even try to hit the monster, knowing its immunity to bullets. Instead he aimed a shot at the handle of the ax. The rubber bullet could not cut through the metal handle, but it packed enough wallop to knock the tool out of the ogre's clutches.

At virtually the same moment, Señor Luis Gonzalez, leaning around Scorchy, fired his huge revolver directly at the ogre's featureless face.

It is quite likely that the excited little detective did not take careful aim, not having either the time or the coolness of mind to have done so. His shot, then, was a remarkably lucky one. It caught the volcano devil in the one vulnerable spot in its entire shielded body—*the eye.*

Transparent shielding tinkled and broke.

Scarlet dribbled down over the faceless helmet.

The monster flailed its arms once, then sagged backward and fell heavily against the wall of the chamber, and moved no more.

Stunned silence ensued. Zarkon swung across the roof of the cavern, swinging hand over hand along the length of the steel-armored power-cable, which was attached to the rocky roof by deep-sunk steel brackets. He jumped down on the far side of the ledge and came around to where the monster lay, motionless, blood dripping down its blank visage from the punctured eye-slit.

Scorchy Muldoon and Señor Luis Gonzalez came crowding at his heels, breathless with excitement.

As Nick Naldini and Phoenicia Mulligan came up, Zarkon knelt by the monster and probed with careful fingers around the base of the monster's neckless head.

There was a metallic clink.

Taking hold of the stony head in both hands, Zarkon twisted. The head turned; gleaming metal grooves were now revealed.

"Holy Houdini!" Nick breathed. "It's a helmet of some kind!"

In the next moment the lanky vaudevillian sucked his breath between his teeth, staring with amazement.

Zarkon lifted the helmet off so they could all see the features of the man who had worn it.

CHAPTER 21

The Ogre Unmasked

They crowded around the figure which lay sprawled and lifeless on the rocky ledge. As they recognized the identity of the man who had worn the monster-suit, a different expression appeared on the face of each.

Señor Luis Gonzalez sucked wind between his gold-inlaid teeth, then huffed his breath out slowly, making his straggly mustache flutter. The dwarfish little detective in the loud checked suit looked completely baffled. His pop-eyes flickered from one to another of his companions, as if hoping to find therein legible the answer to the questions that filled him with amazement.

As for Scorchy Muldoon, the bantamweight boxer was blank-faced with astonishment. His mouth framed a silent whistle. He shook his head numbly, as if to jog his wits back to functioning.

"I don't get it," the little Irishman complained. "Jeepers, he was about th' last guy on the whole blamed island *I* woulda guessed t' be the monster!"

Zarkon said nothing. His stern features, usually impassive, looked gloomy. With hooded eyes he looked down at the dead man, and the expression in those magnetic black eyes was not one of satisfaction.

The Man of Mysteries came from a world and age in

which human life, indescribably precious, was growing ever more rare as the race dwindled towards extinction. The leader of Omega strove always to preserve life, not to waste it; even the lives of criminals he spared, whenever possible. He preferred for such men to pay the price of their crimes in accordance with the penalties of law. He never enjoyed executions, even those which were accidental.

Of them all, it was only upon the features of Phoenicia Mulligan that sorrow and pity could readily be discerned. Her lush lips trembled, and a tear hung like a dewdrop from thick lashes.

This was a natural reaction. It was only to be expected of the girl.

For the dead man at their feet was her former fiancé, John James Jones.

Stripping off the protective suit, the Omega men and Señor Luis Gonzalez lugged the dead man out of the cave. They took the other tunnel, the one which led out onto the side of the mountain, rather than the one which opened upon the inner wall of the crater. It would have been quite a feat to lug the corpse up that narrow crater ledge.

Depositing their burden on the mountain slope which overlooked the cabin in which the dead man had lived for the past six months, Zarkon contacted Ace Harrigan on his belt radio and asked him to request of Señor Valdez some native boys to help transport the body back to the village of Tarapaho. They waited for the bearers to arrive, discussing the recent events among themselves.

Scorchy wanted to know why Johnny Jones had dressed up in the monster suit.

"Wuz he tryin' to scare ivverbody off, er what?" asked the belligerent bantamweight of his chief.

Zarkon shook his head. "Being mistaken for the legendary fire-devil was not part of the original plan at all," said the Man from Tomorrow briefly. "The suit was worn as protection against the blistering heat of the lava-bed on the floor of the crater. It's a special garment, made of polymerized spun-glass fiber, using the principle of vacuum-bubble insulation. Heat-suits of this nature are worn in smelting plants, steel mills, and the like. In fact, Jones probably filched this one from one of the Pacific Mining and Minerals steel mills back on the mainland."*

Scorchy looked bewildered. "But, chief, the dang thing was fixed up t' look like it wuz made o' stone!"

"Not so, Scorchy," said Zarkon. "The outer surface of the suit turns brown upon prolonged exposure to extremes of heat, that's all. And a coating of lava 'scum' adhered to it because Jones wore it down in the lava-bed while surveying the extent of the lode."

"You mean a guy in this-here suit could actually wade through molten lava, chief?" demanded Nick Naldini, with pardonable skepticism.

Zarkon indicated that it was quite possible to do so.

"In fact, such protective garments are worn in steel mills because they can resist the most excessive temperatures—even splattering liquid steel," he affirmed.

* A fact later confirmed by Braxton T. Crawley, who acknowledged that an experimental heat-resistant suit had vanished from PM & M's research laboratory during the same weekend that John James Jones was in San Francisco, after filing his survey report on the mineral resources of Rangatoa, asking Phoenicia Mulligan to marry him, and getting his walking papers from her Uncle. A fire, then believed accidental, destroyed the inventor's notes and specifications for the suit and was believed to have consumed the working model itself. The inventor himself had recently died in an auto accident.

"What ees thees lode, Preence?" inquired the Luzonian detective.

"It's an almost-one-hundred-per-cent-pure deposit of radium, weighing half a ton or slightly more," answered Zarkon. "The largest radium deposit ever discovered, it is worth many millions—especially because it is something like ninety-seven-per-cent-pure radium metal. Most radium discovered up to now has been in extremely impure states, found mixed with pitchblende. To extract and refine the radioactive substance is costly, very dangerous to the health of the workers, and a lengthy and time-consuming process."

"Cripes, chief, I didn't think they wuz much call f'r radium, anymore," muttered Scorchy.

"Not so," Zarkon said quietly. "Its use in medical research, in the prevention of cancerous tissue growth, and a variety of industrial processes make it still very much in demand. Radium as pure as this can be virtually used 'as is,' it only requires being melted into ingot form. I would estimate the value of the deposit as being in the neighborhood of one hundred and twenty-two million dollars."

"But what the heck's *radium* doing on a volcanic island?" demanded Scorchy. "Dunno much about geology, but ivverthing out here's either coral atolls or volcanic—igneous, isn't that th' word? Never heard a radium being found in th' Pacific before!"

Zarkon agreed.

"I cannot say for certain," he murmured, "but I expect that when competent geologists get a chance to examine the site, they will confirm my suspicions that the radium came from an enormous meteorite which struck the island in prehistoric times, lodging within the wall of the crater. That would explain the lack of impurities in the deposit, for one thing. Passage through the atmosphere burnt up the contaminating minerals by simple friction. Radium, in such pure metallic form, has an extraordinarily high melting point.

The notion of a meteorite made of pure radium fascinated the Irish fighter. His eyes glistened at the very thought.

"Jeez," he breathed. "No wonder Johnny Jones wanted t' keep the secret all t' his lonesome. Say, chief—did he find the meteorite when he was here before, when he wuz workin' f'r PM and M? Or only after he quit and came out here, hopin' t' find his fortune?"

"We shall probably never know the answer to that question, Scorchy," said Zarkon.

The native boys arrived, carrying a crude stretcher upon which to transport the body back to the village.

Once back in Tarapaho, everybody clustered around, wide-eyed with curiosity. There were more questions to answer, and Prince Zarkon had to repeat a lot of the information he had already imparted to Nick Naldini, Scorchy Muldoon, and Señor Luis Gonzalez.

Finally, the crowd was dispersed by Señor Valdez, who served a very late lunch to his guests on the veranda of the trading-post, which had only been slightly damaged in the fire. Phoenicia Mulligan absented herself, pleading lack of appetite.

After the meal, over tea, the Omega men discussed the mystery.

"I bet the chief was onto Johnny Jones from the first," Doc Jenkins grinned knowingly. Turning to Braxton T. Crawley, he said: "Chief, here, usually keeps his mouth shut and doesn't let on. But at any point in one o' these shindigs of ours, he's about three jumps ahead a the rest of us. How's about it, chief?"

Zarkon shook his head. "Not from the first, no, Doc. But I had an inkling of the truth from the night he came stumbling into the feast on the beach and collapsed."

"Huh?" Menlo Parker spoke up, incredulous. "Howzzat?"

"As soon as I examined him, I was puzzled," Zarkon explained. "Exhaustion, shock, and exposure can certainly waste a man dreadfully. But not to such an extreme extent, or in such a short time. Especially when one is young, robust, and healthy, as John James Jones reputedly was."

"I don't getcha, chief," complained Menlo peevishly. "What *was* the kid sick of, then?"

Zarkon looked solemn, and his even tones were somber and thoughtful as he replied to the skinny scientist's query.

"He was suffering from prolonged and repeated exposure to an unshielded, powerful source of radioactivity," said the Lord of the Unknown. "That was the only explanation for his emaciated condition."

"Radiation poisonin'?" barked Scorchy with amazement in his voice. "Cripes, chief, I thought this guy wuz a geologist! How come he din't know th' danger o' that deadly stuff?"

"He did," commented Zarkon, broodingly. "But human nature got in the way of his caution. He made the perfectly logical mistake of assuming the heat-suit, with which he could wade through molten lava in complete comfort and safety, was sufficient protection against radioactivity. It isn't, of course. Polymerized spun-glass fiber affords not the slightest protection against radiation. For six months, more or less, John James Jones had been killing himself bit by bit, while gloating over his deadly treasure. . . ."

CHAPTER 22

The Gift of the Island

The Luzon police came in a motor-launch to take custody of the body of the young geologist, to gather the statements of all concerned, and to collect Señor Luis Gonzalez. The dwarfish little detective made his effusive farewells to them all, and returned to the big island with his men, leaving Prince Zarkon and the Omega men with a few loose ends to tie up before they themselves returned home to Knickerbocker City in the *Skyrocket*.

One of these loose ends was the final disposition of the radium meteorite. On this point, Braxton T. Crawley permitted himself to be talked into relinquishing his firm's claim in the mineral rights to the island, in favor of the Rangatoa Islanders themselves. The fat, red-faced man with the enormous mustache puffed and cussed and wheezed, but finally let his niece sweet-talk him into tearing up the mineral-rights option Pacific Mining & Minerals had signed half a year ago.

Under Zarkon's watchful eye, the rotund industrialist drew up another agreement, with more liberal terms. Under the terms of this second document, Pacific Mining & Minerals would develop and market the radium deposit, but the islanders themselves retained complete ownership of their own mineral resources. They would very soon become incredibly wealthy, down to the last tiny toddler in the village.

Zarkon himself arranged for the bank in Mantilla to oversee the island's new wealth. It would be spent, carefully and intelligently and in small parcels, over the years, to build a church, a school, a medical clinic, and other facilities here on Rangatoa. And there would still be plenty of money to insure the higher education or business enterprises of any of the islanders who might wish to avail themselves of these opportunities. Señor Felipe Valdez expressed himself as being thoroughly satisfied with these arrangements.

While his men were getting their gear together, taking their farewells of the islanders, and gathering some souvenirs of the adventure, Prince Zarkon strolled up the beach beside the lagoon to where Phoenicia Mulligan was sitting, kicking her heels moodily.

The blond girl had been silent and depressed ever since the discovery of the identity of the murderous monster. Now she seemed to be coming out of her glum mood, more or less. A sensitive, emotional girl, Fooey Mulligan was also hardheaded and sensible. She was not at all the sort to moon and mope over what cannot be helped. On the other hand, it must have been pretty tough for her to adjust to the fact that the man she had been engaged to was a murdering fiend.

Zarkon tactfully attempted to ease her gloomy mood.

"You know, Miss Mulligan, Johnny Jones never intended trying to kill anyone. He didn't even try to scare people by wearing that suit. Everything that happened was purely accidental and unpremeditated," he said.

The import of his words was astonishing. Phoenicia

Mulligan paled to the lips, turning wide, amazed eyes upon him.

"What—?"

"It's true." He nodded. "When Tommy Kahua caught Jones in the act of emerging from the volcano crater, Jones only intended to quiet him. I am convinced of the fact. He grabbed the native boy for the purpose of silencing his yells. He would probably have bribed him to keep the secret. But he forgot, in the excitement of the moment, that he had just been down in the lake of lava at the crater's floor, and that the gloves of his suit were covered with red-hot lava. His very touch burned the boy to death. But it was completely accidental."

Relief shone in the girl's blue eyes.

"Oh, Prince Zarkon, if only I could believe that!" she breathed faintly.

"You can," he said quietly, "because it is true."

Privately, he himself was not at all convinced. But white lies hurt little. And the relief in the girl's distraught face made it all worthwhile.

A bit later his men joined him at the dock, just about ready to shove off. Ace was already in the big experimental rocket-plane, giving her a preflight checkover.

"Chief, howcum you didn't slap the bracelets on Johnny Jones the minute you figgered as how he was th' ogre?" demanded Scorchy, who had been chewing on this problem ever since it had occurred to him.

"I had no evidence that Jones was the ogre, although it seemed a likely assumption," explained the Ultimate Man. "At first, all I knew was that Jones had a serious case of radiation poisoning. That did not necessarily imply that he was mixed up in the murders. There were any number of ways he could have contacted radiation poisoning without being the guilty party. So I laid a little trap for him."

Scorchy blinked.

"Trap? *What* trap?"

"The heat-suit in the equipment case. Remember, just before we retired for the night, I announced my intention of using it to go down inside the crater the following morning?"

"Yeah," said Scorchy vaguely.

"I was standing outside the room in which Jones had been put to bed when I made the remark," explained Zarkon quietly. "I said it loudly enough for him to hear, in case he was still awake. I had given him a strong sedative, but, as I expected, he had only held it in his mouth until I left the room, then spat it out, into a handkerchief or a napkin. Then, once we were asleep—he climbed out of the window and entered the jungle, where he had concealed the suit just before he came staggering out to collapse at our feast."

"Go on, go on!" gasped Scorchy, to whom this came as complete surprise.

"He pried open the floor and lit an oil-lamp in order to search the equipment-cases and steal or damage the suit I had packed. But in his weak, exhausted condition, Jones was clumsy. He knocked over the lamp. That is what set fire to the trading-post. Seeing what he had done, he got out of there as quickly as possible, hid the suit in the jungle again, and intended returning to his room before his absence could be discovered. He didn't make it in time, so he lay down outside the window to his room, which was full of smoke by that time, pretending to have dragged himself out."

"Cheez," groaned Scorchy to himself. "I shoulda knowed you wuz settin' 'im up! I remember thinkin' as how it just weren't like you t' go blabbin' yer plans all over th' place."

"Precisely," said Zarkon, with a rare smile. "In this particular case, I indeed acted uncharacteristically. I even deliberately lied about my intentions."

"Huh?" blurted Scorchy, incredulous. "*You?*"

"I'm afraid so," chuckled Zarkon dryly. "Because I had no intention of venturing down inside the volcano, next morning or any other time. And for very good reasons, too."

"What reasons is them?" asked Scorchy, ungrammatically.

"There was never any protective insulated suit," confessed Zarkon, "in the equipment-cases in the first place."

The Rangatoans gave Zarkon and his lieutenants a rousing send-off. Señor Felipe Valdez tried to offer the Prince a portion of the island's newfound wealth in payment for his services, but Zarkon declined, politely but firmly. He suggested that if the people of Rangatoa wished to reward him in some manner, they would best please him by donating funds for a new wing to the Savage Memorial Hospital in Mantilla.

Señor Valdez swore to do so; moreover, he vowed that the hospital addition would be named after Prince Zarkon, and that his magnanimity in coming to their assistance would forever be commemorated by a bronze plaque affixed to the new hospital wing. Zarkon expressed himself as being more than satisfied.

Then the islanders did something which took the Man of Mysteries quite by surprise. They presented him with a carved wooden war-club. This signified him as a chieftain of the Rangatoan tribe. And more than that, it was a token which testified to the fact that he was an honorary citizen of Rangatoa, now and forever.

Zarkon said nothing. He accepted the war-club with a peculiar expression on his usually immobile features. Nick Naldini, who stood nearby, smiled gently: the vaudevillian alone sensed how deeply Zarkon was touched by this heart-felt and simple gesture of friendly thanks.

The Prince was a visitor to our world and era, Nick knew. Deep within himself, Zarkon perhaps never entirely felt at home here, but felt himself perpetually the stranger, the outsider. This little act of kindliness and gratitude, Nick recognized, meant more to Zarkon than the man from the future could say. He was more deeply moved by this than by anything that had happened to him within Nick's memory.

It meant that here, on this little island, at least, the Lord of the Unknown was no more a stranger. Here he was at home.

The *Skyrocket* took off with a roar of her engines and soared into the sky. From the deck of the yacht, Phoenicia Mulligan and Braxton T. Crawley waved their farewells for as long as the huge rocket-plane was in sight. Then Phoenicia told her captain to weigh anchor and pick a course for Honolulu.

"Honolulu, is it?" puffed her Uncle, mopping his scarlet brow. "Dang you, gal, but I thought you was comin' back to Frisco with me! Or ain't you got over yer dang foolishness yet?"

Fooey Mulligan looked somber. It was true, she had not quite gotten over her attachment to Johnny Jones. The girl did not give her heart lightly or casually: it would take her some time to recover from this unfortunate love-affair. But then she brightened.

"Uncle Braxton, you don't need to worry about me," said the girl determinedly. "You're gonna have a nephew-in-law yet, and one you'll be proud to acknowledge!"

The fat man groaned. "Who's the pore devil?" he grumbled in his humorous, long-suffering way. "One o' them Omega guys, eh? Thet good-lookin' aviator-feller, I'll bet! How's about it, Fooey? Tell yer ol' Unk! Thet Harrigan feller, is he th' pore soul yew done set yer sights on?"

Fooey pressed her lips shut on a secret smile. Mischief danced in her eyes. But she refused to answer his question.

"Just you wait and see," she said mysteriously.

She went down to her cabin to change into a frock. The fat man watched her go, bemusedly.

Turning to the deck officer who stood nearby, smiling, he said fretfully, "Thet dang-fool niece o' mine! No sooner gets outa one peck o' trouble, then she heads straight fer another!"

The officer shook his head admiringly.

"Miss Mulligan usually gets what she goes after, Mr. Crawley, sir. I wouldn't worry about it, if I were you. Whoever the lucky man is, he's getting a real spitfire, with enough guts, spunk, pluck, and determination for three women!"

Braxton T. Crawley shook his head wordlessly and went waddling off. "Dang thet Fooey, anyway," muttered the fat man to himself as he negotiated the stairs to his cabin. "I wun't even put it past thet gal t' set her sights on Prince Zarkon, hisself!" Struck by the notion, he paused, rubbing his pudgy jaw with fat fingers.

"Wouldn't *thet* just beat all," he mused to himself.

Then, with a hearty chuckle, he went on down the corridor.

"Pore ol' Prince, why, he wun't stand a chance!" he grinned. "Not if Fooey Mulligan makes up 'er mind t' marry 'im!"

Changing into more comfortable clothing, the rotund industrialist continued to chuckle over the wild notion.

"Jest imagine it." He grinned, marveling to himself as he squeezed into the fresh garments. "A gen-*yew*-ine Prince in th' fambly! Wun't thet jest beat all!"

The yacht *Phoenicia* drew up her anchor and got under way. Soon the volcanic island of Rangatoa faded on the horizon, and only the white plume of vapor rising eternally from her smoking mountain remained visible against the darkening sky.

Phoenicia Mulligan had not explained to Braxton T. Crawley her reasons for going to Honolulu rather than to San Francisco. Those reasons, however, were simple. There, at Honolulu International Airport, she could catch a night plane nonstop to Knickerbocker City.

And in Knickerbocker City she fully intended to beard in his den the man who had struck her fancy, and whom she was determined to wed. But whether it was Prince Zarkon or one of the Omega men remains her own secret, although my reader has permission to make a guess of his own.

Postscript

As the *Skyrocket* neared the outskirts of Knickerbocker City, Menlo Parker turned to Prince Zarkon with a question over which the frail physicist had been chewing thoughtfully for some time.

"Hey, chief," demanded the peevish scientist. "Howcum you figgered there was a secret door up on the ledge above Johnny James' hut?"

"There would have to be, Menlo," replied the Man of Mysteries. "Remember the second native boy whom the volcano ogre killed with his burning hands? The first was probably accidental, but the second was deliberate. Jimmie Okawa's body was found way up the slope, on the ledge which zigzagged up to the crest. But there was no reason for him to be up there: he should have gone directly to the hut. The fact that his body was found up on the ledge implied that he had seen something up there which aroused his curiosity, and which he had gone to investigate. That could only be the open door. It could *not* have been the monster. Jimmie Okawa would likely have climbed the slope to investigate an opening where none was known to be; but he would have run away from a sight of the monster."

"Um," said Menlo glumly.

"Okay, now I got a poser for ya, chief," said Doc in his high voice, cheerfully. "How'd'ja figger the radium t' be inside the mountain, when it coulda been anywhere on the island—in the swamp, say, or in the jungle, or anyplace."

"There was no vegetation growing anywhere on the mountain," explained the Ultimate Man. "Volcanic rock quickly erodes into exceptionally fertile soil, as farmers have proven. They have been farming the slopes of Vesuvius since Roman times, despite its record of frequent eruptions. But nothing at all grew on Mount Rangatoa. The deadly radiation shed by the radium deposit could only explain this curious barrenness on an island otherwise thickly grown with lush, tropic vegetation."

"Oh," said Doc thoughtfully.

Nick was looking faintly puzzled, but asked no question. Scorchy gave his lanky compatriot a curious look.

"Spit it out, you half-baked Houdini," he suggested.

"It's nothing, really," muttered Nick.

"C'mon!"

"Oh . . . well, then. It's just that this adventure isn't running true to form."

"Howzzat?"

"You know how it usually works: we got a good-looking gal in one of our cases, and you and I and Ace, say, all go ga-ga over her, but she always ends up giving us the cold shoulder while giving the chief the old glad-eye?"

"Yeah," mused Scorchy, "yer right! Wonder what's wrong with old Fooey Mulligan, anyway! Usually they fall fer th' chief like a ton a bricks!"

Doc, sitting near enough to overhear these mutterings, chuckled.

"You two goons don't think maybe the young lady is still sorrowin' over her boy-friend," suggested the big man with the miracle brain, "even though he turned out to be a crook?"

"Yeah, I guess that's it," said Nick agreeably. But Scorchy wasn't all that sure. A light danced in his eyes and he grinned.

"I dunno, Doc," said the little fighter, gleefully, "I think maybe the chief is losin' his touch with the gals! And maybe Nick 'n' me are in fer some luck in that direction, at last!"

This notion, quite naturally, appealed to the lanky vaudevillian. He rubbed his palms together briskly. "It's about time, too!" he drawled wickedly.

"Yeah," leered Scorchy. "I can hardly wait fer the next adventure t' come along!"

Busy with happy visions, the two said no more during the last leg of their flight to Knickerbocker City.

Of course, they had no idea who would be ringing their doorbell tomorrow morning—a long-legged and very determined blond heiress, who always, but *always*, got her way.

And her man!

THE END

But Zarkon, Lord of the Unknown,
and the Omega men will return in

"THE EARTH-SHAKER."